THE LITTLE LIES

VALERIE KEOGH

BLOODHOUND
— BOOKS —

ALSO BY VALERIE KEOGH

THE DUBLIN MURDER MYSTERIES

No Simple Death

No Obvious Cause

No Past Forgiven

No Memory Lost

No Crime Forgotten

PSYCHOLOGICAL THRILLERS

The Three Women

The Perfect Life

The Deadly Truth

For my brothers, Declan and Brendan.

1

Jodie Armstrong was early. She sat with her cappuccino and stared out the window of the café. There was a good view outside in both directions, she'd be able to see Flynn coming before he saw her, would be able to see if he were ambling along or eating up the path with determined strides. There was so much she would know by looking at him, this man she loved more than life itself.

He was a happy man. He knew some of what she had done to ensure his happiness but he didn't know it all. He couldn't... it was a secret she had to keep. And if there were times in the quiet of the night when it haunted her, when the morning came, she knew she'd do it all again. She was a different person now... love will do that to you, it will turn you into a different version of yourself.

Fate must have been having a laugh the day they met. It had lured them into the same place, watched with glee as they became entwined, then chuckled wickedly as everything began to unravel. But if she could turn back the clock, if she'd known then what she knew now... would she have done things differently?

Lost in her thoughts, Jodie hadn't noticed Flynn coming until the café door opened and he burst through in his usual last-minute rush, a big smile on his strikingly handsome face. He had a sling across his chest and the plump cheeks of the baby tucked inside were rosy from the heat.

'Here you are,' Flynn said, joining her. He undid the sling carefully, unwrapped the baby and passed him across the table to Jodie's waiting hands. 'I'll go and get coffee. Another cappuccino?'

'Please,' she said as she held the baby close to her cheek, inhaling the scent of him.

The queue for service was long and slow. Jodie held the sleeping baby tightly, glancing down at his face now and then, but mostly keeping her eyes on Flynn, the man she loved with every breath she took and every beat of her heart.

Music was playing in the background. Staff, obviously deciding the café was too quiet, turned the volume up as a song Jodie recognised came on. She rocked the baby in her arms and smiled as she hummed along to the old Dean Martin classic, whispering the last words of the refrain, *that's amore*, her eyes softening as she remembered. It had been playing that day she and Flynn had met. A different café. A different time.

If she'd known then what she knew now... the baby in her arms snuffled softly, Jodie cooed soft nonsense words, then looked back to where Flynn was swaying gently in time to the music.

The refrain of the song faded away on the final simple words, *that's amore.*

That's love. That was what it came down to, wasn't it? What you were willing to do for love. She stared at Flynn, the man for whom she'd sacrificed so much, and for whom she'd gladly sacrifice more, and thought back to the first time they'd met...

2

The café on Queen Street had been Jodie's favourite place to stop for coffee in Gravesend, not because the coffee was particularly good, which it was, but they did the most divine pastries. It was her place to go for a treat when life had been tough or tiring, or as it had been that morning, both. It was popular with a lot of people for the same reason, and that day everyone must have had a bad morning because the place was heaving.

The café was too small for the luxury of keeping a table all to yourself and Jodie smiled at the woman who quickly moved her shopping bags to allow Jodie to share her table.

'Thanks,' she said gratefully and put down the tray carrying her filled-to-the-brim cappuccino and custard cream slice before she flopped onto the chair with a sigh.

'No problem.' The woman gave her a sympathetic look. 'You look like you might have had a tough day.'

Jodie was a nurse, virtually every day was tough, some days were simply worse than others. When she'd left her job in Guy's Hospital for a small nursing home in Gravesend, she thought she was taking a step down for a quieter life. It hadn't turned out that way.

It was obvious the woman was waiting for an answer but Jodie wasn't in the mood for conversation. Instead, she pointed towards the custard cream slice. 'It'll be better after I finish this.' She concentrated on her pastry and coffee and a few minutes later she saw the woman gather her bags and leave, murmuring a quiet, *'Goodbye, have a better afternoon'* as she left. Jodie didn't feel guilty. She'd had to deal with a succession of difficult relatives all morning, her store of patience and polite chit-chat was empty.

If she'd hoped to keep the table to herself, though, she was out of luck and within seconds the empty chair was filled. With her pastry gone, she pulled the paperback she was reading from her bag and opened it, folding it back on itself and holding it with one hand as she sipped her coffee with the other.

'That damages the spine, you know.'

A man's voice. Jodie didn't look up. If she ignored him, he'd leave her alone.

'It splits the spine and loosens the pages. Happened to me once, I didn't notice until I got to the last page and found it wasn't there. I was gutted. I had to wait until I went into a book shop to find it and read the end.'

He was speaking as though they were having a conversation, as if they knew each other. Hoping if she kept her head down, she'd freeze him out, Jodie tried to concentrate on her book but she was conscious of the bulk of the man sitting opposite even if she couldn't see his face.

'Must be a good book.'

She looked up then, exasperated, but whatever sharp words were on the tip of her tongue they tumbled off before being said. It had been a difficult shift, she was certainly weary from too many days working with too few staff, but tired and grumpy as she was, she was a woman and not immune to the sight of the gorgeous creature sitting opposite.

Dark hair, brown eyes, and tanned skin, he looked Spanish, maybe Italian and wore a crumpled cotton shirt rolled up at the sleeves to show muscular forearms. His shoulders were broad, the fingers wrapped around his mug unusually long and slim in comparison. And he was smiling at her.

'Yes, it is.' She dropped her eyes back to it, tried to ignore him but she could feel him looking at her and couldn't concentrate. Shutting the book with a snap, she shoved it into her handbag, drained her coffee and put the empty cup down. 'Well, time to go,' she said with a nod his direction, feeling for her jacket, wanting to get up and leave before she did or said anything stupid. Like staying when he asked her to, like saying yes when he offered to get her another coffee, like humming along to the silly Dean Martin song that was playing, and feeling a certain rush of pleasure when he turned to look across the café at her as he stood waiting in the queue.

When he returned with another cappuccino for her and an Americano for himself, he managed to slide his chair a little closer to her. 'Easier to hear you, it's a bit noisy in here.'

'It's not a place for conversation really.' She added sugar to her drink and took a sip. 'You've not been here before obviously or you'd know.'

He shook his head. 'I was here on a work's outing at the Gravesend Golf Club. We played yesterday, I was supposed to play this morning but chickened out and said I'd make my own way home.'

'So, home's not Gravesend then?' The question was out before she could stop it, she hoped he'd see it as natural curiosity, nothing more.

'No, Woolwich. Originally from Bristol though, and you?'

'Living here in Gravesend now, originally from Hampstead.'

5

'What brought you here?' He put his mug down and leaned forwards, looking at her intently as if really interested in her answer.

'I'm a nurse. I worked as a theatre nurse in a hospital in Dubai for several years and when I came home, I got a job in Guy's.' She found herself drowning in his eyes and gave herself a mental kick, dropping her gaze to her coffee and picking it up to take a sip.

'I know Guy's. You're still there?'

He sounded so genuinely interested that Jodie smiled. 'No, I wanted a change and moved into care of the elderly. I work in a nursing home, not far from here.'

'A big change,' he said, echoing her smile. 'Has it worked out for you?'

She put her cup down and shook her head. 'I love what I do but I hadn't anticipated how difficult the job itself would be. We're always short-staffed. The home is part of a big conglomerate. They say the resident comes first and at the same time make decisions that prioritise profit over care. It can be frustrating.'

'I bet.'

His expression and tone of voice were sympathetic but she guessed he probably didn't really understand, not if he worked for a company that took him away for a golfing break. 'Your employer sounds okay. What is it you do?'

'I'm a sales rep for London Medical. It's a pharmaceutical company, the biggest in the city.'

'You like it?'

He shoved his hands in the pockets of his jeans and sat back, stretching his legs out so they almost touched Jodie's. 'I love it. It pays extremely well, there are great perks, to a certain extent I'm my own boss and I get to spend my days meeting and speaking to people, most of whom are delighted to see me.'

I bet they are. The thought leapt into Jodie's head as he finished his coffee and raised a wrist to check the time.

She decided to get the goodbyes in first, draining her coffee quickly and reaching behind for her jacket. 'I'd better be off. Thanks for the coffee. The second one made the difference.'

'Whoever said you can't have too much of a good thing got it wrong.' He tilted his head, his expression serious. 'How about meeting me for a drink sometime, or even better, dinner. There's a good train service between Gravesend and Woolwich.'

The second coffee had sent a caffeine spike to wake Jodie up. This man was gorgeous, but he was way too young for her. There was no point in being stupid. 'I think I'm a little too old for you.'

His laugh was infectious and drew the eyes of every woman in the café, and a couple of the men's.

It drew a reluctant smile from Jodie. 'Perhaps I should have said you were too young for me,' she said, pulling on her jacket.

'How old are you, Methuselah?'

'If I remember correctly, Noah's grandfather was supposed to be nine hundred and sixty-nine. I'm not quite that old yet.' She held her bag to her chest like a shield. 'I'm thirty-four.'

He wagged his head side to side. 'Okay, and I'm twenty-eight. Are you going to deprive us both of what might turn out to be the best relationship we've ever had... either of us... for the sake of six years?'

When he put it like that, it did seem petty. She relaxed her grip on her bag. 'Okay then, let's meet up for a drink and go from there. My name is Jodie Armstrong, by the way.'

'Flynn Douglas.' He held out his hand.

Jodie gave an embarrassed laugh before extending hers. She thought he might push it, hold her hand for too long and make her regret agreeing to meet. But he didn't, he shook it formally and dropped it immediately, leaving her with a faint sensation of loss.

They swopped numbers and arranged a mutually convenient day. 'I'll come to Gravesend for our first date, and maybe you could come to Woolwich for our second.' His smile was mesmerising. 'And for our third...'

'If there's a third.'

'There'll be one,' he said with such certainty that it brought a flush of colour to Jodie's cheeks. She'd never met anyone quite like him before. It wasn't only his physique and good looks, there was something captivating about his smile, about the way he looked at her as if she were someone special.

'There's a pub next door – how about we go there,' she said, getting to her feet. 'Eight o'clock?'

'Perfect. Message me when you're on your way and I'll wait for you outside, okay?'

She should have argued that she could easily have waited inside the pub, that she wasn't helpless, but she didn't, finding his consideration charming. She might as well make the most of it in case, despite his certainty, there wasn't a third date.

As she made her way from the café, she could feel him watching and she concentrated on putting one foot in front of the other without falling over and making a fool of herself. When she was outside, out of his line of vision, she let her breath out in a puff of relief and slumped for a few seconds against a wall before hurrying away in case he came out and saw her.

Her weariness and bad mood had faded to be replaced by sensations that made her float along the path, a smile flitting, brightness in her eyes. The rational part of her was insisting it was a sugar rush from the pastry, but her heart was arguing otherwise... the time spent with Flynn Douglas, that brief meeting... had been magical.

3

Flynn Douglas sat and watched the woman leave. '*Jodie Armstrong*,' he murmured, liking the feel of her name on his lips.

He'd seen her while he was queuing for his coffee, watched her lost in her book as if she were alone in an empty room rather than squashed in a small overcrowded café. She wasn't the type of woman he normally went for; the elegant, sophisticated type who would have given this café a wide berth and certainly wouldn't be tucking into what looked to be a very fattening pastry.

As the queue moved slowly, he continued to stare. Her brown hair was untidily swept into a bun on the back of her head, the T-shirt she was wearing had probably been white at some stage but no longer. But there was something about the curve of her cheek, the arch of her neck, the way she lifted a piece of the pastry with her fork and held it for a second in front of her mouth before her lips parted.

The seat opposite her was vacant. Flynn watched the four people in the queue before him pick up their trays and turn with searching eyes for somewhere to sit and every time he hoped they wouldn't pick that seat. Then it was his turn. He ordered the simplest thing on the menu, a filter coffee, took the mug in his hand and made his way to her table.

She didn't look up as he sat. It gave him time to decide if, close up, she was as interesting as he'd hoped. This near he could see her creamy skin was without makeup. Her fingernails were short and unpainted and she wore no wedding ring. In fact, she wore no jewellery of any kind, not like Carly, the last woman he'd been seeing, with her collection of diamond rings and silver bangles that had to be taken off before they made love. When he'd suggested that maybe she shouldn't put them on, she'd looked at him as though he'd taken leave of his senses. It wasn't surprising the relationship didn't last more than a month.

He wished the woman would lift her head from her book. It would be nice to see her eyes. Flynn sipped his coffee. He needed to say something neutral, not the usual lines he'd try in a bar or a club. He considered the book she was so engrossed in. It was bent back on itself, her hand holding it down as she read. Perfect.

'That damages the spine, you know,' he said, raising his voice to be heard over the general hullabaloo. As an opening gambit it had the advantage of being unusual. But it didn't work, she continued to ignore him. Now more determined, he carried on as if she'd replied. 'It splits the spine and loosens the pages.' He chatted on about his experience but there was still no reaction. He decided to give it one more go. 'It must be a good book.'

She looked up then and his perseverance was rewarded. Her eyes were sunny sky blue. They sparked with irritation for a second before clouding with confusion. He wasn't surprised. He'd felt it too – an instant attraction.

It was so sudden it caught him unawares. Had it been in a bar or a nightclub or any one of the fashionable events he went to, he'd have known how to proceed and would have known the night would end in bed, hers, of course, never his. Never, ever, his. Meeting an interesting woman in a rather downmarket café wasn't something that had ever happened to him before. But he knew he wanted to see her again.

He was delighted when she accepted his offer of coffee and when he queued to get it, he felt her eyes assessing him, much the way he'd assessed her earlier. He wasn't vain, but he knew he was considered handsome, he worked to keep his body in shape and had enough money to spend on a good haircut and expensive clothes. But she wasn't his usual type of girlfriend, maybe she wanted something more than he could provide.

When she'd said he was too young for her, he thought that was it. She was used to older, more worldly, experienced men. He'd made her laugh then, and when she did, he knew she was reconsidering.

So they'd meet for drinks on Friday.

And maybe dinner on Saturday.

And maybe on their third date, they'd end up in her bed.

A frown appeared between Flynn's brown eyes. It might turn out to be the relationship he'd always been looking for.

Did it really matter that he'd lied?

4

Victor Hill had been watching Jodie Armstrong for years, long before she'd moved back to the UK. He'd known from his mother that she'd trained to be a nurse and when he was released from prison, he set about finding her. He tried to find her through the nursing register but to no avail. Prison, however, had taught him patience. He went to Hampstead, to the house where Jodie had grown up. Once there, he reached into his pocket for the container of chilli pepper, dipped a finger into it, rubbed his eyes and with tear-filled reddened eyes, rang the doorbell.

It was answered almost immediately, by a middle-aged woman whose face creased with concern to see a crying man on her doorstep. 'Goodness, are you all right?'

'I'm so sorry,' Victor said, pulling a white cotton handkerchief from his pocket and dabbing his eyes. 'Memories, you know, they can be so traumatic.' He waited to let that sink in. 'My mother passed away recently. You might remember her.' He plucked a name out of the air. 'Sally Winters. She lived the next road down. A tiny woman with a big heart. Everyone knew her.'

The woman hesitated before obviously deciding it was better to lie than upset the crying man further. '*Sally... yes, yes, I think I remember her. I'm so sorry for your loss.*'

'*Thank you. I'm just doing a last walk around the neighbourhood before I head home to Edinburgh.*' He stood back and looked up at the house. '*I have such happy memories of this house. Laurie Armstrong, who lived here some years ago was my mum's dear friend. Mum was very fond of her daughter, Jodie, too. In fact, I was trying to contact her to let her know that Mum had died but I couldn't find an address among her things. It's sad, Jodie will be gutted not to know.*'

As he'd hoped, the woman was only too willing to assist, and as he'd expected, the neighbours still gossiped.

The woman's worried expression lightened. '*Jodie? One of the neighbour's daughters stays in touch with her. She's still nursing, but in Dubai.*'

'*Dubai!*' He'd pasted on a smile. '*What an exciting place.*'

He booked a holiday to Dubai the following week. There were many more hospitals than he'd expected and it took three weeks of painstaking work before he saw Jodie heading through the staff entrance of the American Hospital. After that, it was easy to wait and follow her home. Over the years, he visited several times to keep an eye on her. He had the money, and a holiday in the sunshine of Dubai was no hardship.

He briefly lost track of her when she left Dubai and fell back on a version of the same trick to locate her. Time had passed but memories were long. It was neighbours he tried this time. The first woman he spoke to looked at him blankly before shutting the door.

The next listened to the same tale he'd spun before of a dead mother and his sadness at having lost contact details for Jodie. '*The last address we had for her was in Dubai, but we heard she'd left. Such a shame, I know she'd have wanted to know about Mother.*'

The woman took in his reddened eyes and nodded. 'Everyone loved Jodie. She called around when she came home from Dubai.'

Victor tried not to let his excitement show. 'I don't want to impose and ask for her address but perhaps you could pass on the news for me, the next time you see her.'

'I don't have her address anyway, I'm afraid. And I don't know if she will call again, there's not much here to bring her back apart from memories.' The woman tilted her head. 'I do remember she said she had changed career somewhat. She was tired working in operating theatres and had taken a job in a nursing home in...' The woman frowned in thought, then smiled. 'Gravesend. I remember commenting that it was an unfortunate name for a town with nursing homes.'

Gravesend. Victor had thanked the woman and left. Back home, he'd done an internet search. Four nursing homes in the town. It only took fifteen minutes to find out where Jodie worked. A simple, 'Is Jodie Armstrong on shift today?' getting a negative response in the first two and a positive response in the third. Victor hung up before the call was put through.

It was simple after that. He hung around the nursing home that evening from 5pm. He wasn't sure what position she'd taken so she could be finished at that time but it wasn't until 8.15 that he saw her, a raincoat opened over her navy uniform tunic and trousers. He stepped back into the shadows and watched her walk down the street. She trudged with a weary downward slump to her shoulders and it wasn't difficult to follow her to Wilfred Street. He ducked back around the corner when he saw her stop outside a house and take a key from her pocket. When he looked, seconds later, she had gone inside.

Victor lived too far away to do more than call back the odd day. It was too risky to move closer – there was always the chance she might find out, all she had to do was ask the right person.

Being on the register of sex offenders was a burden he carried with an angry resentment that grew at each refusal to have his name removed. He'd been sceptical when he'd read about a course of treatment in a private clinic and stunned at the cost. But he was lucky; his mother had died while he was in prison and everything she had, including her London house, was left to him. He'd had the house sold as soon as probate had cleared and had left prison with a healthy bank balance. Money, as a result, wasn't an issue. Begrudgingly, he applied to do the course, thinking, rightly as it turned out, that showing willingness to correct his alleged problems would be seen by those who sat in judgement as a good step.

The course of treatment was mundane. Days of excruciatingly boring lectures and one-on-one counselling sessions where he had to chew the inside of his lip in order not to yawn, or worse, laugh hysterically. But the live-in course was held in an old country manor within acres of parkland, the food was excellent and wine, if not precisely plentiful, was at least served with dinner. As in prison, he kept himself to himself and counted down the days.

Twenty-eight days of utter boredom but it had worked. The report stating that he had fully engaged with treatment went with the application to have his name removed from the register and, this time, it was successful.

The same day it was removed, he'd packed his belongings and headed to Gravesend. His needs were simple: prison had taught him a complete disregard for possessions, and a cheap bedsit suited him fine.

Over the next few weeks, Victor watched and followed, took notes, and worked out Jodie's duty rota. It was easy then. He saw her almost every day, walking behind her on the way to work, sometimes waiting until she came off-duty and following her home.

When, on sunny days, he noticed that the front door of the nursing home was frequently left open, it was too tempting to take his observation a step further. He checked the weather forecast, tallied the sunnier days against Jodie's shift pattern and chose a day. When it came, he bought a cheap bunch of flowers, walked through the front door and approached the reception desk with a confident smile.

'Do I need to sign in?' he asked, holding the bouquet of flowers *high enough for the woman to see before burying his nose in it as if mesmerised by the wonderful fragrance.*

'Yes, please,' she said pointing towards the end of the high counter.

'I hope it's okay to bring in flowers,' he said, side-stepping along to the register. He held the attached pen in his hand, as if waiting for her reply, his eyes quickly scanning the names on the page. 'They really are rather lovely,' he said, holding the bunch towards her, hiding his sleight of hand as he turned a page back and skimmed over the names until he found what he wanted. The name of a resident who hadn't had any visitors for a couple of days. 'They're for Elsie Gleeson. She was a friend of my mother who died recently. I promised her I'd come and visit.'

'How lovely,' the receptionist had said, leaning forward to sniff the flowers. 'She'll love them, and we have no restrictions. Do you know where to go?'

He shook his head. 'No, it's my first visit.'

'Room eight, ground floor, the last room on the left. She should be there at this time of the day.'

And it was as easy as that. Elsie Gleeson, delighted with the flowers and the company, professed to remember the deceased Sally Winters well, Victor using the same made-up name for convenience. Elsie was also delighted when Victor asked if he could come again. By his fifth visit, he was on first-name terms with some of the care staff and had even smiled at Jodie when he passed her in the corridor.

He found out all he could about her, followed her to the cafés she frequented, to the pubs where she met her friends, even to the cinema, taking a seat nearby, his eyes on her rather than the screen. It became the best part of his dreary life, the only part that had any meaning.

There was no real plan to his obsession. He was content to be around her, to know what she was doing. Her life didn't appear to be very much more exciting than his, and for that he was strangely grateful. Not even the occasional romantic interlude impacted. They never, after all, lasted long.

That day... the day everything changed... he followed her into the café, stood in the queue one person behind her and ordered food and a pot of tea. He didn't bother with a disguise. She'd never recognise him. Why would she, he'd changed a lot from the gangly, immature, round-faced young man she'd met so many years before.

He spotted a free seat in the corner of the café at a table where two elderly women were setting the world to rights over a small coffee. They'd looked at him askance when he'd asked if the seat was free. He could see it was on the tip of their tongues to lie and say they were waiting for a friend or any of the many excuses they could have used, but instead they'd huffed and puffed and moved their bags and coats from it with less than good grace and lots of drama. When he sat, they huddled closer and ignored him.

It suited him. He wasn't there for the chat, he was there only for Jodie. As usual, she kept her head down, never one for making polite small talk with strangers. He saw an older woman sitting opposite her try, saw her quickly give up when she got no response and leave a moment later. It amused Victor how well he knew her.

He looked at the vacant seat opposite her and wondered about taking the opportunity himself. He'd slide onto it, start a conversation and remind her about their shared past. They might even become friends. He pinned on his best smile, the one that made him look almost handsome, and shuffled to the edge of the chair preparing to stand and take that first colossal step. There was little space to manoeuvre in the crowded café. Awkwardly, with his hands flat on the table, he levered himself upwards, then froze and sat heavily as if his legs had been chopped off at the knee. It startled the two women opposite. They pushed away their long-empty cups, gathered their multiple belongings and left, throwing him wary glances as they did.

'Weirdo,' one muttered, the word falling into one of those sudden silences that occur for no reason, causing her friend to giggle nervously and grab her arm to pull her along. Both hurried to the exit and were gone before Victor had even noticed. He'd not heard the

insult, nor would he have been bothered if he had. He'd been called a lot worse.

Anyway, he wasn't interested in the two women. What had abruptly changed his plans and held his gaze was the man who had taken the free seat opposite Jodie. He wasn't surprised. Jodie was still beautiful but then she'd not had the life of hardship he had. Over the years, Victor had seen lots of men try to lure her into conversation, had smiled at her blunt knock-backs and snickered when the men had skulked off embarrassed. It would happen here too, Victor was sure of it. This man wasn't her type. Handsome but in an obvious way. Too young for her too. She needed a mature man. Someone to take her away from the daily grind of her job.

Victor waited for her to blank the stranger. In the surrounding din, he couldn't hear what the man said but he could see his lips move. And he saw by the sudden stiffness in Jodie's shoulders that she'd heard him but was choosing to ignore. Only someone who knew her as well as Victor did would have seen the signs.

The man didn't give up though. Victor's lips curled at the arrogance. Didn't he understand? Jodie was never going to fall for the likes of him. He watched as the man spoke again and again, watched with growing excitement as Jodie looked up. She'd send the whippersnapper on his way with a flea in his ear.

Victor wished he had sat closer, wished he could hear what it was the man had said because Jodie didn't chase him away. She smiled at him.

A painful dart of irritation faded when Victor saw the man stand, but it returned, sharper, stabbing deeper when the man went to the counter to queue up and Jodie turned her head to watch him. Unable to see her expression, Victor was lost as to what was happening. A few minutes later the man returned to the table carrying two coffees. Victor could see both their expressions again, their smiles, their doe-eyed looks. Irritation was swamped by a tide of anger that clenched *his gut, doubling him over with a groan that attracted startled looks from nearby tables.*

He ignored them, and sat with his arms wrapped around his belly, watching as she laughed and flirted with the strange man. A bead of blood appeared on Victor's lip but he kept biting down on it, the pain focusing him and keeping the anger under control.

The lilt of her laughter drifted across to add a vicious acid burn to the anger. She needed to learn where her future lay.

Perhaps it was time to teach her.

5

Jodie and Flynn went on three dates in quick succession. The Friday night meeting for drinks leading to dinner on Saturday and Sunday. Jodie was bemused by her feelings for Flynn. It wasn't simply because he was so good to look at, it was a connection she'd never felt with any man she'd ever dated. She wasn't normally given to airy-fairy stuff, but it was something almost mystical.

'I feel the same,' he'd said when she tried to explain. 'Almost from the first moment I saw you, I knew I had to be with you.'

From any other guy she'd met, Jodie would have assumed they were simply trying to get her into bed but Flynn was different, she knew he was. For starters, he wasn't pressing her to sleep with him. In fact, when she'd explained that she was working an early shift on Sunday, he'd insisted that they ate early in Gravesend on the Saturday, after which he walked her home and kissed her gently on the lips before leaving to catch the train home.

On Sunday afternoon, they'd met in London and gone for a stroll along the embankment, holding hands, stopping now and then to kiss like teenagers. Jodie was working a twelve-hour shift on the Monday, so once again, they'd had an early dinner. Afterwards, he'd walked her to her train and waved till it was out of sight.

Feeling blissfully content, Jodie rested her shoulder against the window. She was oblivious to the city as it trundled past, seeing only Flynn's face in her mind's eye, and when her phone beeped, she smiled, knowing it was him.

Missing you already xxx

Me too xxx

She put her phone away and rested her head back. Two twelve-hour shifts to work until she was free on Wednesday and she'd see him that night. In Gravesend. Dinner at an Italian restaurant not far from her house on Wilfred Street. It had been her choice, she knew what she was doing. Flynn was the best thing that had happened to her in a long time, maybe ever. What was she waiting for?

Monday turned out to be a nightmare. Of the six care assistants who were supposed to be on shift in the nursing home that day, three rang in sick. The night nurse had done her best, had rung every member of staff who wasn't working to beg them to come in and managed to get one. Only when the night nurse had tried everyone, was she allowed to call an agency. By that stage it was after seven, the shift started at eight and any agency staff available had already been allocated work.

A twelve-hour shift with two staff less than she should have was a nightmare. Jodie filled in where she could but even working flat out, corners were cut. The manager, Katy Dobson, was sympathetic and told Jodie she was doing a great job before she toddled back to her office and shut the door.

To add to Jodie's woes, there appeared to be more visitors than usual, family and friends who all wanted to discuss the care of their nearest and dearest. She managed to swallow a mug of coffee as she wrote up her notes but she didn't have time for lunch or supper. When the cheery voice of the night nurse signalled the end of Jodie's shift, she was ready to collapse.

The nursing home was only a fifteen-minute walk from the terraced house she'd bought when she returned from Dubai. After living in rented accommodation for so long, she wanted, finally, to have her own place and had fallen in love with the extended and renovated house as soon as she'd viewed it. She put an offer in the same day and moved in less than two months later.

That night she trudged home, the walk seeming endless. When she couldn't find her keys in the muddle of stuff in her bag, she started to cry, weary tears of frustration that further hampered her search. Finally, as she was about to empty the contents of her bag onto the path, her fingers closed around metal and she pulled out the keys.

Inside, she went upstairs to the bathroom, threw her uniform in the laundry basket, and had a quick shower to wash away the stress of the day. It helped a little, as did the soft comfort of the robe she wrapped herself in before going barefoot down the stairs. She needed to eat; another twelve-hour shift loomed the following day. According to the roster, she had a full complement of staff but that could change before the morning.

Too tired to bother with any effort, she took a tub of hummus from the fridge, grabbed a teaspoon, and went into the sitting room. There was a street light almost directly outside her house and it shone through the gauzy voile panels that covered the windows and lit up the room, throwing strange shades and shadows over the walls. She put the hummus and spoon on the coffee table and stepped over to pull the heavy curtains.

Through the voile she had a hazy view across the street outside, only a narrow path separating her front door from the road. The building at the end of the road was a church of some unusual denomination. When services were on groups of people would often pass by on their way to or fro, but at this time of night the church was shut and the road was quiet. She pulled the curtain, blinked in the darkness, and stepped carefully towards where a lamp stood on a small table in the corner of the room.

The sofa she'd bought when she moved in was a tad too big for the room but it had been the most comfortable she'd tried and she'd wanted it. She sank onto it, curling her legs underneath and reached for the remote control to switch on the TV.

The hummus was almost gone and Jodie's eyes were growing heavy when the house phone rang, startling her. She wasn't expecting anyone to call. A brief hope that it might be Flynn quickly fizzled. He didn't know her home number. It could be her friend, Rivka. She'd not spoken to her for a few days. She glanced at the ornate clock that stood on the mantelpiece. Ten o'clock. Her friend would never ring that late. When it stopped, she shrugged. Probably a wrong number.

That thought hadn't finished when the phone rang again. Someone definitely wanted to get hold of her. She reached for the handset. 'Hello?'

'Jodie, it's Katy Dobson.'

Jodie swung her feet to the floor. 'Katy? Is something wrong?' Because there had to be. Ringing her at home, at this hour, something had to be wrong.

'I'm sorry, Jodie, I'm afraid I'm going to have to suspend you pending an investigation.'

Jodie laughed because she couldn't think of any other way to react. Suspended? 'What am I supposed to have done?'

'Bessie rang me. There's been a serious medication error. I'm sorry, I've been left with no choice.'

Bessie, the smiling, helpful night nurse. Why hadn't she rung Jodie if she'd discovered a problem? It was bound to be something she could clear up easily. Jodie didn't make medication errors, ever. But a complaint had been made and the wheels would go round and round. 'Okay, I understand. What happens now?'

'I'll be in touch regarding a meeting with you and the human resources manager. You're in the RCN, aren't you?'

Jodie murmured an affirmative, grateful she'd taken the advice to join the nursing union.

'It might be a good idea to contact them. I have no choice but to inform the NMC, the RCN will be able to deal with that for you.'

Jodie felt a tightness in her chest. If the Nursing and Midwifery Council was involved, this was serious indeed. 'Can you tell me what the error was?' The day had been manic, had she done something wrong?

'Bessie found medication on the bedside locker in room six.'

Room six. Daisy Courtland's room. Jodie frowned. That couldn't be right. 'Daisy isn't on any regular medication.'

'Exactly!' There was a note of triumph in the manager's voice as if Jodie had admitted her fault.

Jodie's head was spinning. 'I don't understand...'

'I'll be in contact with you over the next couple of days to arrange a date for the preliminary investigation.' Katy hung up without another word.

Shock kept Jodie immobile, the handset clasped in her hand,

a rigid expression of fear and self-doubt on her face. Had she left someone else's medication in room six accidentally? The bedridden Daisy didn't take any medication, unusual in a woman of ninety-three. But when Jodie was doing her medication round, she always called in to say hello. Had she put a medicine pot down on her locker by mistake? She shut her eyes in horror. If she had, it meant that another resident hadn't received their medication.

For the next couple of hours, she went over and over as much as she could remember of the day. It had been crazy. Medication rounds were supposed to be protected, staff weren't supposed to call her for assistance, residents weren't supposed to ask for help and their families weren't supposed to want to talk to her. But all of those things happened. And on a day they were short-staffed, they'd happened even more. But she was an experienced nurse, she could cope. And she didn't make mistakes. Did she?

Did she?

Maybe if she knew what medication had been left, she might be able to figure out whose it was, and how she could have made such a ghastly error. Because it had to have been her. She was the only person who gave out medication. It had to have been her... the thought was devastating. She loved being a nurse, she didn't want it to end like this.

The phone was still in her hand. She could ring and ask Bessie what medication she'd found. But Jodie knew she wouldn't. Bessie hadn't shown much solidarity by ringing Katy rather than her.

It was after midnight before Jodie went to bed, and nearly three before she fell into a restless sleep where tablets of various shapes and sizes grew wide gaping mouths that screamed abuse at her for what she'd done.

She sat up with a start at seven, then flopped back with a

hand over her eyes. She didn't have to go to work that day, might never have to go to work again. Fifteen years a nurse and she'd never made an error. Never had as much as a reprimand. Warm, silent tears of self-pity slid from the corner of her eyes.

There didn't seem any point in getting dressed either so she pulled a robe on and headed downstairs. The extension that housed the kitchen had taken up most of the small garden but the previous owner had made the most of what little space there was, and a small window to one side of the room overlooked a pretty courtyard. Jodie had been lucky. Because the owner had been going abroad, he'd been happy to leave several large pots filled with a variety of plants including some very elegant acers. As September rolled on, some of the flowers were fading but several vibrant geraniums continued to add a splash of colour.

There was space in front of the window for a table and chairs. Unable to find ones small enough in traditional furniture shops, Jodie had had the bright idea to buy garden furniture. And the white wrought-iron set she'd found – a table and two chairs – fitted perfectly.

She made a pot of tea and sat drinking it while she looked out the window and tried not to think of what had happened. There was no point in going over it again and again until she knew all the facts. As soon as it hit nine, she'd phone her union and see what advice they had to offer her.

Meanwhile, only another nurse would understand, so early though it was she rang Rivka, her go-to friend in times of crisis. She and her partner tended to be up at first light so Jodie wasn't afraid of disturbing her.

Rivka's reaction to the sad tale was heartening: a long silence was followed by a grunt of disbelief. 'You're kidding me, aren't you? You don't make mistakes, you're a dot every I, cross every T kind of woman.'

It made Jodie out to be terribly boring and predictable but

she appreciated her friend's sentiments. 'They're saying that yesterday I wasn't quite so efficient.'

'Right, well, I'm not working today, I'll be straight over.'

'No, thank you,' Jodie said quickly. 'Honestly, I'm fine. Being able to talk about it with someone who understands is enough. I'm going to ring the RCN and see what they say. Then I'm going to treat the rest of the day like an unexpected day off and laze around reading and watching TV.' She managed to inject so much enthusiasm into her plans for the day that she almost succeeded in fooling herself.

'If you're sure.' Rivka didn't seem quite convinced. 'Ring me if you hear anything or if you want to chat, okay? I'm here for you. And keep your chin up, you're a brilliant nurse, remember that.'

'Thanks, that's what I needed to hear.' Jodie hung up with a smile that faded as she picked up her mobile and did an internet search for the RCN phone number.

Her union was as efficient and supportive as she'd expected. They assured her that if she wanted a rep to attend the investigative meeting with her, one would be provided and spoke about it as if it was all routine. Perhaps it was to them, but to Jodie it was a horrifying nightmare. She was always so sure of herself, of her competence. Now that was being called into question and even though she knew she'd done nothing wrong... doubts were beginning to creep in. She had been overworked, stretched too much, she knew corners were being cut... had she made a mistake?

Weighed down by worry, she sat in a daze for several minutes, then picked up her phone and sent Flynn a text.

Are you free for a chat?

She held the phone in her hand, hoping for a reply and when it came, she drew a shuddering breath.

Give me five minutes

True to his word, five minutes later, her phone buzzed and she heard Flynn's deep, steady voice saying *hello* and suddenly her worries were a little less frightening.

'Hi,' she said. 'I hope I didn't drag you away from anything important.'

'No, it's fine. You okay? You're not cancelling tomorrow, I hope.'

'No, it's not that.' Now that she was speaking to him, she wasn't sure why she'd rung. What did she expect him to say? He wouldn't understand anyway. 'I'm having a bad day, work-wise and wanted to hear a friendly voice.' It wasn't exactly the truth, but it wasn't a lie either.

'Oh, poor you.' His quick sympathy brought a lump to her throat. This had been a bad idea, she was going to start bawling any moment.

'I'll tell you all about it when I see you tomorrow. I'd better go, thanks for getting back to me, that was all I needed. Bye.' She hung up, but she didn't bawl. Flynn Douglas was good for her. A brief chat with him had done what the conversation with her union had failed to do, it had given her back her belief in herself.

She'd done nothing wrong. When she went to the meeting with Katy and the human resources manager, she'd prove it.

6

Jodie spent the rest of that Tuesday keeping herself busy. She washed the inside of all the windows, changed the bed linen, put a wash on, and did the pile of ironing that had built up over the last week, feeling resolute as she ironed her uniforms. She'd be needing them again soon.

Rivka rang late afternoon. 'You doing okay?'

'More positive, thanks. It's all a load of nonsense, it'll be sorted. I'm not going to worry about it anymore.'

'That's the spirit! Honestly, we have enough crap to deal with without adding to it. When I told Tasha, she was horrified. I'd only been talking about you recently, telling her what a brilliant nurse you are.'

Jodie smiled. She'd seen Tasha's eyes glaze over when Rivka and Jodie drifted down nursing memory lane and could picture her rolling her eyes to be told what a great nurse Jodie was. It was hard for a girlfriend of two years to understand a platonic friendship of eighteen.

They chatted for another thirty minutes and by the time Jodie put the phone down she was convinced she'd made a fuss about nothing.

It was a frame of mind that stayed with her, allowing a more comfortable night's rest and when she woke in the morning and panic fluttered through her mind, she was able to squash it down. *Down, not away.*

If her upbeat mood required a lot of propping, she thought that was okay too. And she'd have managed to keep strong if she hadn't come down the stairs to see the white envelope sitting on the floor by the front door.

She did everything online so post was an increasing rarity. Approaching it warily, as if it was going to fly upward and slice her to ribbons with its sharp edges, she looked down and recognised the logo of the nursing home across the top of the envelope.

The upbeat mood, forced as it was, didn't have a chance to survive the official words of the letter informing her that she was under investigation for gross misconduct. She'd been stupidly optimistic. This was serious. Gross misconduct was a firing offence, and an offence the NMC would take very seriously. She could be struck off the register. What would she do then? Nursing was all she'd ever known, all she'd ever wanted to do.

She sat and read the letter. The meeting was to be held the next day at eleven. She was entitled, it stated, to bring her union representative with her, or to choose to be accompanied by a friend.

A friend. She could ask Rivka; she'd take a day off work to help her. But Jodie shook her head. Strangely, although she'd known him such a short period of time, she knew exactly who she wanted by her side. She picked up her phone to tap out a quick message. *Can you take tomorrow morning off?*

It was over an hour later before her phone buzzed. She stared at it, willing it to have the answer she wanted, sighing in satisfaction when she read, *Sounds like a good plan.*

Flynn had agreed without even asking why. Okay, he

probably was thinking of a night of passion followed by a relaxing breakfast somewhere rather than being dragged to an investigatory meeting. She'd explain that night over dinner but she knew he wouldn't let her down. It was odd how she knew she could trust him completely.

Unwilling to spend the day mooching around the house worrying, Jodie ran back upstairs. Twenty minutes later, she was back down wearing comfortable clothes and her walking shoes. Fresh air and exercise would help keep her sane.

She decided to have breakfast along the way and stopped at the first café she came to on Harmer Street. The prospect of the next day's meeting was the perfect excuse for indulging so she ordered her favourite – smoked salmon and scrambled egg on sourdough toast washed down with a large cappuccino. When it arrived, looking delicious, she discovered that worry wasn't a good aperitif. She ate a few mouthfuls before pushing it away and a few minutes later, without finishing her coffee, she left.

The sky was a cloudless blue, the temperature warm enough for Jodie to take off and carry her light jacket as she walked along Gordon Promenade and the Thames and Medway Canal, but she pulled it on again when she reached the flat, exposed Saxon Shore Way, turning her collar up to protect her from the chilly breeze that blew across the broad expanse of the Thames. Sometimes, she'd walk only as far as Shornemead Fort but today she kept going to Cliffe Fort. Over a ten-mile walk there and back, it would give her the exercise she needed and, if she were lucky, it might calm her rattled brain.

Both abandoned buildings were disused artillery forts and neither held much allure but the views across the river, and back towards Gravesend, were worth the walk and usually she'd stand and stare, but not that day. Despite her hopes that exercise would lighten her mood, it didn't appear to be working.

After four hours she arrived home, tired and philosophical.

The next day she'd know what the case against her was and be able to address it, until then, she was driving herself crazy thinking about it.

She'd also been mulling over what to tell Flynn. Or more to the point, when to tell him. Finally, she decided she wasn't going to say anything until the morning. She was going to have a good evening, she was going to sleep with her gorgeous boyfriend for the first time and nothing was going to interfere with that.

With that thought firmly set in her head, she had a long shower and spent more time than usual choosing what to wear. She pulled out a dress she'd bought a few months before, slipped it on and smoothed the fabric over her hips. It felt good and the colour suited her.

She left her hair loose, applied a lick of mascara and a pale-pink lipstick and she was ready. Too early, of course, and for the next twenty minutes she sat staring at the TV. For the first time since that Monday night phone call, she wasn't thinking about the horrendous situation she'd been thrown into. Instead, she fizzed with anticipation.

When her doorbell rang at six on the button, despite expecting it, she jumped. She giggled nervously then, reminded herself that she wasn't sixteen and answered the door with a relaxed smile pinned in place. 'Hello,' she said, standing back and waving him inside, quivering with surprise when instead of passing, his hand snaked around her waist and pulled her close to him. She could feel the heat of his hand through the fine material of her dress, the heat spreading as his lips came down on hers.

An hour later, Jodie sat up in bed and looked down on the sleeping man beside her, a smile playing on her lips. Wow! She liked sex, had few if any inhibitions and had had numerous lovers over the years, but without a doubt Flynn was the best, most giving lover she'd ever had.

His eyes opened and he turned to look at her. His expression was serious, intent. 'You are something else,' he said softly.

'I was thinking much the same about you.' She pushed her tangled hair back from her face. 'Luckily, the restaurant I've booked is very easy about reservations, they'll have kept our table.' She grinned down at him. 'Suddenly, I'm ravenous.' Leaning forward, she kissed him lightly on the mouth, then swung her legs from the bed. 'Give me ten minutes and the bathroom is all yours.'

'We could shower together, save time and water.'

Her laugh was deep and earthy. 'I somehow doubt it would save time. No, I'll be out in five and you can have it.' Euphoria sent her floating across the landing, happiness kept her smiling as she hopped under the jet of hot water. No sooner in, she was out and wrapping a towel around herself.

She opened the door to find Flynn standing there, his nakedness taking her breath away and making her weak with longing. Maybe they should stay home, make love all night and all day tomorrow; she could forget about the meeting, forget about everything except this unbelievably beautiful man. She could... but she couldn't.

'I'll go get dressed,' she said, reaching up to plant a kiss on his cheek.

They walked hand in hand to the restaurant. As Jodie had expected, the staff made no comment on their being an hour and a half late, greeting her with obvious pleasure before showing them to their table.

'You come here a lot, I gather,' Flynn said, taking his seat.

'It's close, it's good, so yes, I suppose I do. Actually,' she amended, 'I usually get a takeaway. Sometimes if friends come to visit, I'll take them here but more often we'll meet in the city.'

They ordered wine and food and sat sipping the wine when it arrived and chatted about nothing in particular. It was only when the food was finished and the second bottle half-drunk that Flynn put his glass down and reached across the table to clasp her hand.

'We hardly know each other but strangely I feel something's troubling you.' He squeezed her hand gently. 'If you don't want to talk about it, it's fine, but I am a good listener.'

She thought she'd been doing such a good job hiding her worry about the next day. The amazing sex, the lovely evening, and more wine than she normally drank had certainly pushed it to a tiny corner of her mind but now and then she could feel it reminding her it hadn't gone away.

'It's a work issue,' she said, trying to make light of it.

'Tell me.' His eyes intent on hers, his hand still holding hers tightly.

She shrugged, took a sip of her wine, and gave him a quick summary of the accusation against her.

Flynn frowned. 'Okay, so this resident... Daisy... she doesn't take medication, you were merely dropping in on her to see she was comfortable?'

'Yes, that's it. She doesn't see many people during the day especially if we're busy so I like to drop in when I can.'

'But you were under pressure, would it be a case that you had the next person's medication in your hand and put it down for a second to speak to Daisy and simply forgot about it?'

It was one of the scenarios Jodie had considered. It would have been so unlike her to be that careless but she supposed it was possible.

'This Daisy–' Flynn was still mulling over it '–would she have been likely to have picked them up and taken them?'

'No, poor Daisy has arthritic fingers, she'd not be able to pick up anything even if she were able to reach over her bedrails.'

'Well then!' He released her hand and spread both of his in a *what's all the fuss about* gesture. 'Sounds like they're making a big to-do about nothing.'

'Yes,' Jodie agreed and smiled at him. He hadn't a clue how bad this could be, there was no point in trying to explain, no point in ruining the rest of the night. Anyway, she'd reconsidered her decision to take him to the meeting. It wasn't appropriate, they might see it as belittling the seriousness of the situation. More importantly, if everything went wrong, if she had made a colossal error, she didn't want Flynn to see her as less than the ideal nurse, less than the perfect person she wanted to be in his eyes. 'I'm probably making way too much of it. I'm going to a meeting with the manager tomorrow, it'll probably all be sorted.'

'Of course it will be. There'll be a reasonable explanation and they'll apologise for putting you through so much grief.' He reached for her hand again. 'I'm glad I was here for you though.'

Jodie returned the pressure of his hand. She'd made light of it. It wasn't a *meeting with the manager,* it was a formal disciplinary procedure which could have huge implications for her career. But sitting there with Flynn, it didn't seem quite so frightening.

The wine was gone, the restaurant empty, the staff throwing furtive looks in their direction. 'We should go,' Jodie said, putting her hand up when Flynn reached for his wallet. 'No, it's my turn to pay, remember.'

Minutes later, they were outside in the dry chilly night. Flynn draped an arm around her shoulder, pulled her close and they walked the short distance to her house with the comfortable familiarity of a couple who'd been doing the same journey for years.

In bed, they explored each other's bodies, discovered what each liked, loved, wasn't keen on, laughing at the latter as they made love through the night, falling asleep and waking in a delicious cycle of desire.

When Jodie woke again, she saw a line of light around the edges of the blackout curtains. Her brain wanted to start preparing for the meeting at eleven; her heart wanted to dwell on the warm body next to her, the arm resting heavily across her abdomen and the soft snore that came rhythmically from the face almost buried in a pillow beside her.

Her brain won.

She pushed Flynn's arm off, shaking her head at the childish hope that she'd disturb him and he'd reach for her, taking the choice away. Childish and stupid. She had no idea what time it was, it certainly wouldn't do to be late for this damn meeting. Flynn gave a soft grunt and changed position as she slid from the bed. Seconds later his rhythmic breathing resumed.

It would have been blissful, had she been able to stay there staring at him. He really was a beautiful man.

She grabbed her robe from the back of the door and headed downstairs to where the big kitchen clock told her that, at a minute past nine, she'd plenty of time to spare. Her phone was in her handbag where she'd dropped it the previous night when there had been talk of coffee that had never materialised, both realising that the only stimulant each needed didn't lie in caffeine. She smiled and pulled out her phone to check for messages. There was one from Rivka asking if she was okay and wondering if she were still alive. Jodie sent a reassuring reply, promising to ring later.

She rang her union to ask if it was too late to organise a rep to go with her that morning. Unfortunately, it was. Advised to reschedule the meeting to allow them to organise someone to attend, she shook her head. 'No, thank you, it's fine. I'd prefer to get it over with.'

She sat at the table to prepare herself for the meeting, but as she stared out over the courtyard all she could think of was what she'd do if she lost her job. There would be time to do the work outside she'd been planning to do for months – rearrange the pots, plant some spring bulbs, maybe paint the wall. If she lost her job...

'Hi.'

Her head jerked around. 'Hi, yourself.'

Flynn was dressed, looking remarkably good in jeans and a crumpled T-shirt.

'You want to have a shower?'

He shook his head and held up his mobile. 'A potential client I've been trying to get hold of for weeks is finally available.' He pulled at his T-shirt. 'I'd planned to work from home this afternoon, hence the casual gear. Now I have to go home and change.'

'Poor you!' She stood, stepped closer to slide her arms around his waist and rested her head on his chest. She wasn't small but her five six was dwarfed by his six two. 'Shall I make you some coffee before you go?' His arms closed about her and she felt his lips on her forehead.

'No, I'm good. I'll get one at the train station.'

He didn't move away. She breathed in the very faint whiff of body odour, the lingering hint of his aftershave and wanted to ask when she'd see him again, pressing her lips together to stop the words escaping. They weren't teenagers, she was old enough to have sense, to know that she should take it slowly, to have learnt how to play the damn game after so many years.

'You free on Friday?'

Friday. Two days away. The day after the next day. Of course she

37

was free. She was about to say she was when it dawned on her that she didn't know. It was her weekend to work, a horrendous three twelve-hour shifts back-to-back Friday to Sunday. But that depended on that morning's meeting. What was it Flynn had said? That it was a big to-do about nothing. If he was right, she'd be working on Friday and too exhausted to do anything afterward, not with a twelve-hour shift the next day. 'It depends on how the meeting goes today,' she said. 'If it goes well, I'll be working all weekend.'

'Well,' he said, 'in that case, you'll be working.' He kissed her cheek. 'Knock 'em dead today. I'll ring you after my meeting and we can plan to meet up next week.'

With another kiss, this time firmly on her lips, he was gone.

Jodie stood at the door waving till he was out of sight. It was something her mother used to do, stand at their garden gate every morning and wave as Jodie went off to school. The memory made her smile. She stood there until a man passing on the other side of the street shot her a strange look, then wrapping her robe tighter about her, she stepped back and shut the door.

7

Victor had been standing around the corner of the church on Wilfred Street watching Jodie's house when he saw the man come out and he immediately recognised him as the same man she'd met in the café on Tuesday. Irritatingly handsome, annoyingly overconfident, he strode down the street with the kind of self-assured arrogance that made Victor want to heave. He guessed they'd met a few times since the café, fornicating in animal lust while he was busy making plans.

When the man was out of view, Victor strolled down the street on the opposite side. He saw Jodie in the doorway, oblivious to his regard. Her robe was partially undone, hair unbrushed, lips slightly swollen from a night of passion. His nose twitched – he swore he could smell the stink of sex polluting the air as he walked past. In his pockets, his hands clenched into fists.

Oh, but she'd learn, he thought, reaching the end of the road.

Peering around the corner of the building, Victor was sorry there was no sign of lover boy. He'd have liked to have followed him, snooped around to find out who he was, where he lived, whether he was hiding a partner and children somewhere while he was screwing around with Jodie. That there was something off about him, Victor was convinced. He'd seen it the first day in the café, something odd that he couldn't quite figure out. But he'd figure it out eventually. Persistence – like patience – paid in the long run.

Victor retraced his steps, passed the church, and crossed the road. From this angle, he could see the front of Jodie's house, but there was no chance of her seeing him.

She never saw him. Had probably forgotten about his existence. Soon that was going to change. Soon she'd be forced to remember. He'd make sure of that.

8

At ten thirty, Jodie stepped out and locked the front door behind her. She'd chosen her clothes with care and hoped the navy trousers, white shirt and pale-blue linen jacket made her look efficient and professional, not the kind of person who'd have made a silly error about anything.

She carried a large tote with a notebook and pen inside to take notes. It seemed like the right thing to do. This whole situation was so outside anything she'd ever known that she felt queasy, a sensation that increased as she neared the nursing home.

There was a keypad to the side of the door and she pressed the four-digit code without thinking, her hand raised to push the door as soon as she heard the beep. But it didn't come. She bit back a grunt of frustration and tried again, pressing each key slowly. It wasn't till the fourth attempt that realisation slammed her across her face. The entrance code had been changed. She'd worked at the home for six years, it had been the same code the whole time. Was it too much of a coincidence that she'd been accused of a serious medication error and the code had been changed? Or was she a little paranoid?

She glanced at the time. Ten minutes to eleven. She needed to get a grip on her rising panic. A few steps took her to a small garden where a stone seat was set amongst tall ornamental grasses. It was all for effect and she'd never seen anyone from the home using it but it was the ideal place to spend a few minutes. She sat on the cold stone and listened to the breeze shushing through the grasses behind her, a hypnotic sound that helped settle her nerves.

At two minutes to eleven, she returned and rang the front doorbell, waiting for it to be answered as if it was all routine, even managing a smile for Audrey the receptionist who pulled the door open with a concerned expression on her normally jovial face.

'Good morning.' Jodie was pleased to hear her voice sounding normal, strong and firm. No sign of the tremor she could feel in her belly.

'Oh Jodie.' The oozing sympathy in Audrey's voice was almost her undoing. She'd hoped the error she was being accused of would be kept confidential, making it easier to return to work with some level of authority, but if the receptionist, the home's town crier, knew about it, then everyone did.

Audrey's eyes were bright with curiosity as they searched Jodie's face for signs of her devastation, for anything to gossip about in hushed whispers over coffee later. It was time for Jodie to brazen it out, she mightn't stop the gossip, but she could change the script. She gave a shrug indicating, she hoped, her unconcern at this silly situation and her total confidence she would be cleared of any wrongdoing.

A door opened to the right of the reception area to instantly claim both women's attention. Audrey scooted back behind her desk and Jodie, with a lift of her chin, turned to face the manager.

'Good morning, Jodie,' Katy Dobson said, standing back and waving into the office behind her. 'Come in, please.'

The office was spacious and bright. A floor-to-ceiling window on one side overlooked the garden where Jodie had sat only moments before, the arching flower spikes of the grasses directly outside providing some privacy for both room and garden.

There were two other people present. Jodie recognised the dumpy woman with the overlarge glasses perched on the end of a pert nose as Ivy Skellin, the human resources manager. The other woman, staring at her with suspicious, almost condemnatory eyes, was a stranger.

Katy sat behind her desk and nodded to the remaining vacant chair. 'Have a seat.'

Jodie sat. She'd have liked to have hugged her bag to her chest in protection. Instead, she opened it, took out her notebook and pen, dropped the bag to the floor beside her and sat back expectantly.

'This is a preliminary investigative meeting to discuss the allegation against you.' Katy linked her hands on the desk in front of her. 'You know Ivy, of course, and this–' she waved towards where the second woman sat '–is Ms Youlden from the company's legal team.'

Jodie's smile to both wasn't returned. She kept it pinned in place for a while longer before letting it fade away.

'At the end of this meeting, we will ask you to wait outside while we discuss how to proceed and let you know our decision.' Katy unclasped her hands and met Jodie's eyes. 'Do you have any questions?'

Tension had risen at the very officious nature of the meeting and tightened almost unbearably at the mention of someone from the company's legal team. Jodie had never had much time for the huge conglomerate, BestLife Care, who spoke about residents' care coming first while refusing to provide the money or facilities to ensure it did. But if they'd sent a legal representative, they were taking this situation very seriously indeed.

'I'd like to know the details of the allegation against me,' she said, tapping her pen against the notepad.

The manager opened the file in front of her and took out a sheet of paper. She ran her eyes over it, her eyes widening as if shocked, as if reading it for the first time. It was an affectation – Jodie knew she would have read it several times before this meeting.

Katy held the page up by the corner, her mouth twisting as if disgusted by what was written there. 'This is Nurse Bessie Abbott's statement.' She placed the page on the desk and adjusted the glasses that sat on the edge of her snub nose. 'On the night of Monday 16th September,' she read aloud, 'I, Bessie Abbott, the registered night nurse, did a routine check of all the residents following handover from the day staff nurse, Jodie Armstrong. In room six, I approached the sleeping Daisy Courtland to check she was comfortable, then turned to exit the room. I spotted a medicine pot on her bedside locker. Surprised to find it half full with medication, I removed it and took it to the treatment room. To my horror–' Katy looked up from the sheet and caught Jodie's gaze. Without looking down at the page, she continued '–I discovered that there were several different pills in the container, ranging from cardiac to diuretic. I followed protocol and rang the manager.' Katy looked towards the other two women. 'Following which, *I* immediately suspended Ms Armstrong.'

The world was buckling under Jodie, she wanted to throw her notepad and pen down and grip the sides of the chair. This couldn't be happening. There was no reason that several pills would be in a medicine pot in Daisy's room. None at all.

She felt the stickiness of perspiration in her armpits, the cold sweat of fear on her forehead. 'I don't understand.'

The manager withdrew another sheet of paper. 'We did a medication audit. It was checked and double-checked.' She slid the report across the desk. 'That's a copy of the results.'

Jodie picked it up, but the numbers and words danced on the page.

'As you can see,' Katy explained, 'the medication in stock tallies with medication received and dispersed.'

Worse, far worse than Jodie had expected. She kept her eyes on the page as if she were reading, her mind whirling in a void. She had no explanation. There was none.

The woman from the legal team lifted a hand and waved an index finger between herself and the human resources manager. 'Perhaps you could explain the implication of that to us, Katy.'

The manager tapped the report. 'Since everything tallies, how do we explain the medicine pot of medication?' She looked across the desk, her face pinched into lines of disdain. 'The only explanation is that some medication wasn't dispensed to the residents during the day. But there is another, and far more sinister side to this. And that is why were the tablets found in Daisy's room?' She let that thought float around the room before picking up yet another sheet of paper. 'I spoke to one of the care assistants,' she said, putting the sheet down and looking back to Jodie. 'She said that on the Monday morning you stated that Mrs Courtland had no quality of life, is that correct?'

Jodie heard the indrawn gasps from the others and felt herself go cold. Katy's insinuation that Jodie had planned to give the medication to poor Daisy was breathtaking. There was no need to ask who the care assistant was. A woman a little older than Jodie who'd started work in the home only a few months before. New to care work, her previous employment having been in the retail sector, she'd been on a lengthy induction and was reasonably adept. But her attitude was appalling. Only a wet week in the place and while still on induction, she was telling other more experienced staff what to do. Jodie had noticed too, that she was nicer and kinder to the residents when their family members were present. Jodie remembered the conversation she'd had with her, remembered asking her to spend more time with the less fortunate of their residents, those who had nobody to visit. They'd been near room six at the time and Jodie had indicated the room as an example. She *had* said poor Daisy had no quality of life, but that was only a part of the sentence.

'I remember telling one of the care staff that Mrs Courtland had no quality of life unless we ensured she had by spending time with her, sitting with her when we could, trying to engage with her.' She lifted her chin. 'It sounds like your care assistant has a very selective memory.'

'She is a very valued member of the team,' Katy said, 'but since we're discussing selective memories, what are your thoughts on why a container of medication was found in Mrs Courtland's room?'

'Could they have been left there the previous day?' Ivy Skellin spoke into the silence.

Jodie's eyes brightened. Of course, that must be it. Not her fault at all.

But Katy shook her head emphatically. 'I spoke to the housekeeper who checked with the household staff. The person who cleaned the room that day said she'd not seen anything out of the way and furthermore says that had she seen medication lying around she would have brought it to the nurse's attention immediately.'

Jodie felt all eyes focus on her. Were they expecting her to launch into a confession? To say that, yes, she'd held back several residents' medications, and kept them to give to poor Daisy to help her shuffle off this mortal coil? To admit she'd done that, then was so unbelievably stupid that instead of giving them she left them sitting there for someone to find? To admit to being that incompetent?

She drew a breath and let it out then, calmly, with her chin in the air and exaggerated emphasis on certain words, she spoke. '*Every* resident in my care, was given the *correct* medication, at the *correct* time. I have *no* idea how or why medication was found in Mrs Courtland's room except to state without a hint of doubt, they were *not* left there by me.'

'Did you leave the medication keys unattended at any stage during your shift?'

Jodie looked across the room to where the legal representative sat with her legs crossed, painted, manicured nails tapping the notepad balanced on her knee. Was she offering Jodie a way out? She grasped at it but felt the immediate sting. It wouldn't work, because even if, by some wild flight of fancy, some unknown person got their hands on her keys and withdrew medication from her trolley, how would they account for the medication audit tallying?

'No, I didn't. They were in my pocket at all times until I handed them over to the night nurse.' She looked from one to the other deliberately. 'I am careful with all aspects of medication. I know the importance and don't make errors.'

'Nevertheless, medication *was* found where it shouldn't have been.' Katy looked towards the other women. 'Do you have any further questions?'

Both shook their heads. 'If you'd wait outside for a few minutes, Ms Armstrong, we can discuss how we're going to proceed.'

Jodie grabbed hold of the notebook she'd not written a word in, picked up her handbag and left the room.

Audrey was busy on the phone but her eyes followed Jodie as she walked across the reception to the front door. She'd have liked to have waited outside but she didn't know the code to get back in.

She'd reached the door and was considering what to do when the door behind opened once more. Their considerations hadn't taken long. Jodie hoped that was a good sign.

'We're ready.'

There wasn't much to be learned from Katy's closed expression. Nor was there any clarity on the faces of the other two women who looked Jodie's way when she entered. She sat in the same chair, this time keeping her handbag on her knee. There didn't seem to be any reason to take out her notebook, even if there was something to write she wasn't sure her trembling hands would be able to grasp a pen.

'This is a grave matter,' Katy began. 'We did wonder if we should involve the police but since we have no proof of any criminal intent, we decided it wasn't in the home's interest.' She nodded towards Ms Youlden in acknowledgement of what had to have been her input. 'But in view of the seriousness of what has occurred, we have no choice but to terminate your employment forthwith.'

Jodie felt the blood rush from her face and peripheries in a mad dash to shore up her heart which she thought might have stopped. She refused to faint in front of this triad of condemnatory women.

'You are entitled to your holiday payment but, as of today, you are no longer in the employment of BestLife Care. We will be letting the NMC know of our decision and there is no doubt that they will carry out their own investigation.'

Of course they would, and if Jodie were found guilty by the governing body, she might be suspended or worse, struck off and never be able to work as a registered nurse again.

There was nothing more to be said. No gratitude for the six years of unblemished service Jodie had given, the long hours, the unpaid overtime, the soul-destroying days when staff was short and the work unending. She left the office, shut the door behind her and took one step after the other across the reception to the front door. Somewhere, as if at a great distance, she heard her name called. She didn't know who was calling, or why, or care, simply kept going, out the door, through the car park, out onto the footpath, then onward to home.

It was hours later, time spent curled up on the sofa with her arms wrapped around herself and tears falling unheeded, when a thought came to her. She knew she hadn't left the tablets in Daisy's room.

But somebody had.

9

Strangely, rather than panicking, the idea that someone had deliberately framed her for the medication error, made Jodie sit up and think.

If she were right, if someone had done such a terrible thing, surely it would be easy to prove. Her eyes flicked to the clock. Rivka would be home. She pulled her bag across and took out her phone, smiling when she saw messages from Flynn. Three of them.

Hope the meeting goes well, xx

Followed by:

Thinking of you, xx

And finally:

Let me know how it went, will be free by five, ring me, xxx

She would ring him, but first she needed to speak to Rivka,

she might be able to help. How, Jodie wasn't sure, but she had great faith in her friend's abilities. If it could be done, Rivka would be the one to do it.

Her phone was answered on the first ring, her friend's breathy *How did it go* tumbling out before she'd a chance to say hello.

'Ghastly! Worse than I could possibly have imagined.' Jodie filled her in on the meeting and the accusation against her. 'They've fired me.'

'Bloody hell! Can they do that?'

'Unfortunately, yes, since they're accusing me of gross misconduct and putting residents' health at risk. Never mind that they virtually accused me of having designs on a resident's life.'

'Bloody hell!'

Jodie was almost amused. She couldn't remember her friend being stuck for words before. 'Since I know I didn't leave those blasted tablets there, it looks like I've been set up.'

'Set up?'

It was an improvement on *bloody hell* but still not much help to have Rivka parroting everything she said. 'It has to be that,' Jodie said firmly. 'I didn't leave the tablets there and nobody else has access to medication during the day, so someone had to have brought them in and left them there.'

There was silence from the other end.

'Rivka?'

'Yes, I'm here, thinking. This is some seriously creepy stuff you're saying. If you're right, someone deliberately set out to ruin your career but who would do such a thing?'

'I don't know.' Jodie had considered and rejected any of the staff she worked with, even that irritating care assistant. Irritating and incredibly stupid, but not vindictive or malicious. Jodie's leaving wouldn't impact very much on anyone really.

She'd never fallen out with anyone, never had words with any of the residents' families. 'As far as I can think, nobody would have a motive for doing such a thing.'

'Troublemakers don't always have a motive, though, do they? Maybe you pissed off that care assistant more than you think.'

'I work with her maybe once or twice a month, I can't see it really.'

'Then who?'

'I don't know. I'll speak to my union tomorrow and see what they think. I was wondering about fingerprints.'

'Fingerprints!' Rivka's voice rose in a squeak. 'Seriously?'

Jodie moved the phone to her other ear and rested her head back. 'If they could lift fingerprints from the medicine pot, they'd know they weren't mine and I'd be in the clear, wouldn't I?'

'I suppose.' Rivka didn't, however, sound convinced. 'I hate to burst your Sherlock Holmes bubble, but what are the chances they kept it? If it was a reusable pot, it would be washed and back in service and if it was a disposable one, it's in the rubbish. The tablets will be in an envelope, signed, sealed and locked away.'

Jodie groaned. 'Okay, you're right, of course. But what else can I do?' A hint of desperation crept into her voice. 'If I can't nurse, what will I do? It's all I've ever done.'

'Talk to your union tomorrow. Be guided by whatever they say, this is what they do after all. Have you looked at the amount of people who go before the NMC panel? Almost a hundred a month and most are given suspensions or conditions of practice orders. You don't see the cases that are simply dismissed, because their details are immediately removed, but I bet there are a lot.'

'Mine won't be dismissed,' Jodie said. 'However, those tablets got there and whoever put them there – they were there, and I was in charge, so the blame will be put firmly on my shoulders.'

'Maybe a condition of practice order then, some medication training–'

Jodie's harsh laugh interrupted her. 'Having someone looking over my shoulder for months, doesn't that sound jolly!'

'If it means you can stay nursing it will be worth it. You know how much you love your job,' Rivka reasoned, always the practical one.

Sometimes the voice of reason was what you needed to hear. 'Yes,' Jodie said wearily. 'But it's not going to be easy.

'I hate to be trite, but nothing worthwhile ever is. You'll get through this and I'll be with you all the way, okay?'

Rivka hadn't come up with a magical winning formula to make everything all right but she would be there for Jodie, and if things went completely belly-up, she'd still be there, she always was.

'I know you will, thank you.' Promising to ring her the following day, Jodie hung up.

She stared at her phone. It made sense to ring her union straightaway but she couldn't bring herself to have that conversation. Instead, she rang Flynn.

'Hi,' he said, answering immediately as if he'd been waiting for her call.

She smiled at the thought, feeling some of the tension easing. 'Hi, yourself.'

'How did it go? I bet it was a storm in a teacup.'

'They fired me.' If she said the words often enough, she supposed they'd start to feel real. She'd been fired. She waited for his response, expecting disbelief, horror, and words of sympathy, so when laughter pealed down the phone, she dropped it as if it had bitten her.

10

A t the end of Wilfred Street, Victor paced. He'd followed Jodie to the nursing home earlier, noting her rather formal attire and set, grim expression. From the corner of the gateway, he'd watched as she pressed the front door access key unsuccessfully. When she turned away, her lips were clamped together, eyes downcast. She stumbled a few steps, swerving to enter the small garden to the front of the building. After sitting there for a few minutes, she returned to the front door, this time ignoring the keypad and ringing the bell.

He'd liked to have been able to follow but although he'd been into the nursing home several times, he didn't want to risk being uncovered at this stage. Instead, he went into the garden Jodie had taken shelter in, sat on the same stone bench, and looked around. It was a pretty spot. He'd have been happy enough to have sat there waiting for her to come out but when he turned around to admire the plants behind him, he couldn't believe his luck. There she was! The fronds of the grass offered sufficient shelter for a shadowy man to conceal himself. He stood as close as he dared. A light had been switched on inside the room and the four women stood out in sharp relief against the white walls. Jodie sat the far side, slightly forward so she wasn't blocked by two women he didn't recognise. The woman seated behind the desk, he knew to be the manager, Katy Dobson. Victor smiled. It was amazing how much a quiet unobtrusive man could find out without asking questions.

He couldn't hear anything, but years in prison had taught him the bitter lesson of anticipating what might be heading his way by reading the slight change in expression that foretold danger. Necessity made him a quick learner and before the first bruises had healed, he'd acquired some skill. By the end of his prison sentence, not only had he become adept at reading expressions, but he'd learned the importance of blending into the background, of sliding through the day unnoticed. It was a façade he cultivated carefully even after he was released on parole.

From where he stood, the two women's faces nearest him were hidden, but he could see Jodie's profile and the manager's face. The manager's expression was disdainful, disappointed, angry, and as hers became more entrenched, so Jodie's became more beaten and subdued.

Victor smiled again. It looked like Jodie was in trouble.

11

Jodie stared at the phone in disbelief until into the silence she heard her name called, a hint of panic in Flynn's voice. She leaned over, scrabbled on the floor for the phone and picked it up. 'Sorry, I dropped it.'

'Jodie, oh God, I'm so sorry. I laughed because I really thought you were pulling my leg. How can they have fired you? You did nothing wrong.'

'No, I didn't. I have to keep reminding myself of that. Not that it matters. I was the nurse in charge. Medication was discovered where it shouldn't have been. I'm being accused of gross misconduct.'

'But... surely you're innocent till proven guilty.'

It was her turn to laugh, a bitter sound that seemed to echo around the room. 'It appears not,' she said. 'They have to act in the best interest of the residents, blah, blah, blah.'

'But that's ridiculous.'

'There'll be an NMC investigation too, I could be struck off.'

'What! What's an NMC?'

Jodie wanted sympathy not an interrogation. 'It's the Nursing and Midwifery Council, the governing body. They'll investigate and decide if I'm allowed to continue nursing or whether I'm such a danger that I should be struck off.' She could hear the deafening sound of defeat in her voice. 'They may let me work until they're finished their investigation or may tell me I can't. I'll ring my union tomorrow, they'll be able to find out for me.'

'I'm coming over,' Flynn said. 'Sit tight, I'll be there as soon as I can.'

She didn't argue. Letting the phone drop to the sofa beside her, she rested her head back and shut her eyes as tears stung and trickled. She'd not moved when the doorbell chimed an hour later.

'I can't believe this,' Flynn said as soon as she opened the door. He stepped inside, dropped a bulging holdall, and took her in his arms.

It was good there, warm and safe and the key to release the tension that had gripped Jodie since the meeting. Within seconds, she was sobbing.

Flynn did what he should. He held her without saying a word until, finally, she hiccupped and was quiet. She didn't move, though, his arms were wrapped around her, holding her together. She took comfort in their strength.

'What can I do?' His lips brushed her hair.

'You did it,' she said, pulling away reluctantly. 'Coming here and being with me, that was what I needed. Thank you.' She looked down at the bag he'd dropped. 'Looks like you're planning on staying a while too.'

'Sounded like you needed me, sounds like you're going to for a while.' He brushed hair back from her cheeks and tucked it behind her ears. 'I like to be needed.'

'I'm not sure I like being so needy, but it's just for today. I'll talk to the union tomorrow and see what the next step will be.' Together they walked to the kitchen where Jodie filled the kettle and switched it on. 'I'm hoping they'll allow me to work otherwise I'll be sitting around for months twiddling my thumbs.'

Flynn propped himself against a wall as she filled mugs with coffee and poured water and milk. 'How will you manage if they don't let you work? How will you pay the rent?'

Jodie handed him a mug and waved towards the sitting room. Once she was sitting on the sofa, the mug cupped between her hands, she answered him. 'I'm lucky. I don't rent nor do I have a mortgage. I used money I saved when I was in Dubai along with an inheritance from my mother to buy this place. I still have a bit aside.' She smiled slightly. 'I refer to it as my run-away money. You know, if ever life got too boring, it would allow me to simply pack my bags and take off. I was thinking of getting bored, though, not fired.'

'At least that's one thing less for you to have to worry about.' Flynn sipped his coffee. 'Why don't I take you out for dinner. We can have a bottle of wine and talk about what you're going to do.'

Jodie looked down at the shirt and trousers she'd put on that morning. 'Okay, but let me change into something more comfortable.' She pulled at the material of her shirt. 'I was trying to look professional and efficient.'

'You look amazing but change if you want to.'

She put her mug down. 'I'll be a minute.'

In fact, it was fifteen before she returned. She'd had a shower to freshen up and applied heavier makeup to cover the pallor that shocked her when she looked in the mirror. 'Better?'

'You looked wonderful before but you look stunning now.' Flynn stood and put an arm around her waist to pull her close. 'Plus, you smell divine. Maybe we don't need dinner after all.'

Jodie laughed and pushed him away. 'I need food and I most definitely need wine.' She leaned forward and planted a kiss on his cheek. 'But thank you, you've made it all a lot easier.'

~

They went to the Italian for convenience and were in luck getting the last free table. They both went for pizza, agreed on red wine and within minutes were sitting back with a glass in hand.

'Here's to you being cleared of any wrongdoing,' Flynn said, raising his glass to her.

'Amen to that.' Jodie clinked her glass against his. She gulped a mouthful and sat back. 'I needed this.'

'Wine, good food and the company of someone who cares. It's the magical combination when things are a bit rough.'

Jodie tilted her head. 'Sounds like you're speaking from experience, Flynn. Why don't you tell me your sad story to take my thoughts off mine?'

He stared into his glass for a few seconds before shaking his head slowly. 'Maybe another time. Tonight, it's all about you. Tell me, where will you look for a job if that MNC crowd tell you that you can continue working?'

Jodie smiled. 'It's NMC.' The smile faded and she gave a weary shrug. 'Even if they tell me I can work while they're carrying out the investigation, I'll have to tell any prospective employer that the investigation is ongoing. It won't make it impossible to get another position but it may make it difficult.'

'Would you think about doing something else?'

She lifted her glass and swirled the wine around. 'I've been a nurse all my working life. It's all I ever wanted to do. I enjoyed working in operating theatres but when I moved into care of the elderly, I found it much more satisfying.' Her fingers tightened on the stem of the glass. 'It's so unfair.'

Flynn reached across and took hold of her free hand. 'You'll get through this and I'll be here for you while you do.'

Jodie turned her hand and wrapped her fingers around his.

What luck it had been to meet him. With him and Rivka on her side, she'd do okay regardless of the outcome. She picked up her glass and took a drink to hide her suddenly tear-filled eyes. She was kidding herself. If the outcome was bad, if she were really struck off, what *would* she do?

Flynn tried his best to keep her spirits up and she did manage to smile at the funny stories he told her about some of the customers he had to deal with but she was conscious that her smile was forced.

'Thank you,' she said as they walked home hand in hand. 'It would have been a sad evening on my own if you hadn't come over.'

He put an arm around her shoulder and pulled her closer. 'I'll be here for you as long as you need me. It's no problem for me to work from here for a few days. I may need to go back to my place for more clothes but that's all.'

'Maybe I could go with you. We could stay at your place for a while. I could go out to the galleries or go shopping.'

'My apartment is only a studio, didn't I tell you? It's fine for one but definitely not big enough for two.'

'Oh,' Jodie said, surprised. She was under the impression he lived in a spacious apartment but when she thought about it, she couldn't remember if it had been something he'd said or not. They'd reached Wilfred Street and she took out her house keys as they approached the front door. 'It doesn't matter, there's plenty of room here, thank goodness.'

She'd turned from Flynn to put the key in the lock so missed the look of relief that swept across his face.

12

The wine, food and company had done its best to ease Jodie's distress but as soon as the lights went out and she was left once again to her thoughts, it came barrelling back. She turned her head to look at the sleeping man beside her, trying to focus on him, on his kindness, his understanding, his acceptance that sex wasn't on the cards that night. He'd held her in his arms and she'd stayed there until she heard his breathing change to a slow, deeper rhythm, then she eased from his arms and lay back against her pillow.

The puzzle of the medication haunted her. She knew she hadn't left it there. The housekeeping staff were diligent, though, so had it been there from the day before it would have been reported. It had to have been put there sometime late afternoon. By someone. Someone who wanted to make trouble for her. It was a galling thought that she had someone who disliked... even hated her... that much. It brought the sharp sting of tears to her eyes but she rubbed them away. She'd done enough crying that day.

One step at a time. Tomorrow, she'd ring her union, get their advice, see what the NMC were going to do. She needed to have her wits about her. Sleep was essential, but as soon as the thought swept through her head, anxiety tightened its evil claws rendering sleep impossible. After an hour, she slipped from the bed, pulled on her robe, and crept downstairs.

Sometimes when she couldn't sleep, she'd switch on the TV and watch something mindless but her bedroom was directly above the sitting room, the sound would carry and one of them being awake in the wee hours was enough. Instead, she made herself a mug of camomile tea, took it through and curled up on the sofa. She hadn't bothered to switch on the lights. The heavy curtains had been left open and the room was bathed in a hazy orange glow from the street lights outside.

She tried to keep things in perspective and reminded herself she had done nothing wrong but her head insisted on focusing on the simple fact that she had been fired. The camomile tea wasn't helping at all, maybe something stronger was in order. Alcohol, she knew, wasn't the answer but as she got to her feet and headed to the cabinet where she kept her small supply, she thought it would be a good short-term one.

With a small glass of brandy in her hand, she curled up again. She tried to keep her thoughts on the good things in her life. Her friends, her lovely home, Flynn. But the insistent thought that someone wanted to do her wrong wouldn't go away.

It certainly hadn't gone away after her third brandy but neither had sleep come. Restless, Jodie switched on the lamp beside her and reached for a book she'd been reading. She tried to lose herself in it, the words blurring on the page as alcohol and tiredness took effect. Minutes later the book dropped from her hand as her head bounced once, twice, before slumping on her chest. But even as she registered that she'd at last fallen asleep, her eyes snapped open. And on it went until the orange glow vanished and the colder light of daybreak filled the room.

At seven, she heard the distinct sound of an alarm from the room above followed by the creak of floorboards, the opening and closing of doors and the hum of the electric shower in the bathroom. Comfortable, homely sounds. It had been a long time since she'd shared her living space. Few boyfriends had been invited to spend the night since she'd moved there, she couldn't, in fact, remember the last time. Maybe two or three years before. Certainly, nobody had ever arrived with a huge holdall, intent on staying for the foreseeable. The thought brought a smile to her lips. It felt so right.

She stood and stretched wearily. It was time for coffee, gallons of it. In the kitchen, she set the little table with mugs and plates, switched on the kettle, and made toast, slipping the slices into a rack as they were done. 'Perfect timing,' she said as the door opened.

'Did you get any sleep?' Flynn asked, sliding a hand around her waist, and planting a kiss on her lips. He leaned back. 'You taste of brandy.'

'I hoped it would help but it didn't.' She smiled again and sat at the table. 'Sit, have breakfast before you go.'

They sat in silence for a few minutes. Jodie watched Flynn spread butter thickly on his toast and lace his coffee with three sugars. How he maintained his physique eating like that she didn't know. He was wearing the same charcoal-grey suit he'd worn the day before, the shirt a shade lighter, and a tie with a yellow-and-grey pattern. 'You look good first thing in the morning,' she said, sitting back with her coffee between her hands.

It made him laugh. 'I aim to please.' He brushed crumbs from his tie. 'In my job, you have to look smart otherwise customers... and your competitors... will think you're not doing well.'

She hadn't thought about that. 'Easier for me, I pull on one of my selection of navy uniforms, tie back my hair, and off I go.'

'Much easier,' he said, raising his wrist to check his watch. 'I must go. Good luck with your union today, I'll try to ring you later in between meetings but if I don't get the opportunity I'll be back tonight and you can tell me everything, okay?'

'That's fine,' Jodie said, getting to her feet. 'If the union says it's okay I'll be busy job-hunting anyway.' She reached a hand to brush a crumb from the front of his jacket. 'It will be nice to be able to look forward to seeing you tonight.'

Flynn pulled her into a hug. She felt the strength of his lean body and soaked some of it up to keep her going for the day.

'Stay strong,' he said, and with a final kiss, he opened the door and left.

She waved until he rounded the corner and disappeared from view then shut the door and went back to the kitchen. Her eyes were gritty from tiredness but she knew she'd not be able to sleep until after she'd spoken to the union so she sat and poured the remaining coffee into her mug. It was only eight fifteen and it was unlikely they started work before nine.

Taking her coffee through to the sitting room, she switched on the TV and sat back to watch the breakfast programmes without any real interest, losing focus after only a few minutes. She switched channels, found a rerun of *Friends* that probably had been funny the first or second time she'd seen it several years before but now didn't as much as make her smile. Irritated, she switched off the TV.

Trying to fill in the time, she had a long shower, washed her hair and blow-dried it rather than tying it up wet as she usually did. By the time she was done it was almost nine and she ran downstairs and picked up her phone to dial the number she'd saved.

It was answered almost immediately. When Jodie gave her name, she was told she'd been allocated a representative.

'If you hold, please,' the pleasant voice continued, 'I'll see if he's free to speak to you.'

Jodie listened to the silence, the phone pressed to her ear. 'Hi Jodie,' a deep voice said. 'My name is Taylor Bennet. I'll be handling everything to do with the NMC investigation. I'm sorry I wasn't free to go with you yesterday. Now, tell me everything you remember, everything that happened and was said.'

It didn't take long. 'That's it,' she said finally, slumping a little in her seat.

'And you have no idea how that medication appeared on the bedside table of that resident?'

'Absolutely none.' Her voice was firm. It was the one thing in this mess that she was one hundred per cent clear on.

'Okay. They're not saying that any medication was given in error, and any theories they have seem a tad far-fetched. If you were going to do something dishonest and unprofessional would you have been stupid enough to have left the container of tablets lying around?'

'Exactly!' The same thought had been going round and round Jodie's head since the previous day. 'Someone had to have put them there but, before you ask, I've no idea who'd have done such a terrible thing.'

'Let's not worry about that. Our aim is to clear you, not to find out who was responsible.' There was a crackle of paper before Taylor spoke again. 'You can choose to receive the NMC reports yourself and forward them to me or you can nominate me to receive them directly.'

'Oh yes, please, I'll nominate you,' Jodie hurried to say. The less she had to do with the NMC the better she liked it.

'Okay, I'll send the relevant document for you to sign. Now, do you have any questions?'

'What about getting another job? Is that allowed?'

'Absolutely. You do, as you probably know, need to inform any prospective employer that you're under investigation. Tell them as much as you feel you need to.'

The thought of having to tell an employer that she was under NMC investigation was galling. 'I have savings, I might not bother–'

'If you want to continue nursing,' Taylor interrupted her, 'if you want to put the best case forward, it is in your interest to get another job asap. You'll then be able to get positive feedback so that we can prove you're a good, reliable, efficient nurse and a credit to the profession.'

She had to prove she was what she was. Once again, Jodie felt a bitter twinge at the unfairness of it all. 'Okay then, I'll get another job.'

'Good. Right, we'll keep you informed of our progress. But I will warn you, these things take months so try to get on with your life and don't worry, that's what we're here for.'

Easy words, Jodie thought, hanging up. So damn easy to say, "don't worry", a hell of a lot harder to do.

With another mug of coffee to hand, she fired up her computer and started the job search. When she'd returned from Dubai she rented in the city while she worked in Guy's. It was her decision to move into the care of the elderly that had made her decide to look further afield. She'd chosen Gravesend for several reasons, the proximity to good transport and reasonable house prices being the biggest two. But also for the number of nursing homes in the area. BestLife Care had been the first she'd contacted. They'd responded within days and offered her a position immediately following her interview. And she'd not regretted that till now.

It had been convenient to where she lived, but there were others. Three to be exact. All within half an hour's walk of her home. She looked them up, one after the other, wrote down the details and checked their vacancies, pleased to see that they all had nursing positions available. There was nothing to choose between the three homes. One was slightly nearer maybe. But she knew she couldn't afford to be that fussy.

It was no harm to send an updated CV to each and see what happened. She put her finishing date with BestLife Care as the previous day but no further information. If they wanted to know why she'd left, they'd have to ask her.

A few minutes later, she pressed send, then shut her laptop.

Weariness was a heavy weight pushing her down. She put the laptop on the empty chair, crossed her arms on the table and lay her head down. But sleep wouldn't come.

Frustrated, she got to her feet. It was only eleven. A whole day to fill. Flynn wouldn't be home till five or six, maybe she should cook him a dinner here rather than having to eat out again. And shopping for food and cooking, it would help pass the time. Decision made, she pushed to her feet and trudged up the stairs for her coat and purse, stopping to peer out the bedroom window to assess the weather. Blue skies and sunshine. Something was working in her favour.

She was considering what to cook when she opened her front door and, lost in thought as she was, it took a few seconds before she realised there was something tied to her doorknob. A small box, wrapped in blue paper and tied with a matching wide ribbon, the bow of which was hooked over the knob. She stood staring at it, a frown creasing her forehead. She hadn't ordered anything recently from anywhere and even if she had done, crazy as the delivery companies could be at times, this was surely beyond them.

Her frown faded. Flynn! It had to have been him. He must have got to the train station, bought something, and dashed back to leave it there as a surprise for her. And what a wonderful, thoughtful surprise it was. She was lucky it hadn't been stolen. It was easy to unhook the bow and she lifted the package, looking for a card. There was nothing, nor was there anything written on the paper. She took it inside and shut the door.

Her fingers itched to tear off the ribbon and wrapping to find out what was inside, but half the fun was in the anticipation. Delayed gratification... there was a lot to be said for it. Anyway, the blue ribbon was too pretty to waste. Jodie sat at the kitchen table, undid the bow, and put the ribbon to one side. The box was neatly wrapped, the edges tidy, the joins taped over. It was light too. She shook it but whatever was inside didn't rattle or clink. Something soft? Reluctant to tear the paper, she stood, took a knife from the cutlery drawer, slid it along the join and peeled it back.

Underneath the paper was a plain white box with a lid. With a dart of excitement, Jodie lifted it off. Flynn had gone to a lot of trouble... and expense... the gift was folded in tissue paper. She hoped he hadn't been too extravagant. Taking it out, she smoothed the tissue paper back with her fingers, already smiling in the expectation of finding something pleasing, a smile that froze in place when she saw what it was.

Two little baby shoes. Soft blue fabric. Little straps with tiny pearl buttons holding them shut. A dark-blue heart embroidered on the front of each.

Jodie stared as the blood leached from her face, a shaking hand reaching out to touch first one, then the other, ever so gently as if there was a baby wearing them.

Her baby.

As she picked up the shoes and pressed them to her lips, a long, low keening sound came from a place she'd forgotten, from a time she'd forced herself to forget.

13

Loss, sorrow and deep despair combined to create a heavy numbness that kept Jodie pressed into the chair, unable to move or drop the little shoes. The only thing she seemed to be able to do was blink when her staring eyes grew dry.

The phone rang, and rang off, then a short while later it sounded once more. It was this second persistent noise that made Jodie gulp and move to pick it up. 'Hello.' Her throat was dry and the one word came out as a gravelly whisper. 'Hello,' she tried again.

'Jodie, are you okay? I've been ringing and ringing.' Rivka's voice was tight with concern. 'You promised to ring me, remember? I've been worried.'

Hadn't she spoken to her union rep only minutes before? Jodie looked up at the round red clock that hung over the kitchen door and blinked in disbelief when she saw it was two o'clock. She'd been sitting there for hours. 'Wait,' she managed to say before putting the phone down and struggling to her feet.

She picked up the coffee mug she'd left on the counter and took a mouthful of the cold drink, then sat and picked up the phone again. 'Sorry. I rang my union first thing and spoke to my rep. Then I put my head down and must have fallen asleep.'

'I bet you were awake most of the night worrying,' Rivka said, her voice soft with sympathy. 'Listen, why don't I come over? I'll pick up a couple of cream cakes and we can indulge while you tell me all about it.'

Jodie looked at the baby shoes she still held in one hand. Rivka was her oldest friend, she knew all about her past. Maybe it would be good to talk. 'That would be great. Actually, there's something else I need to talk to you about.'

'Say no more. I'll be over in about an hour.' She hung up without another word.

Jodie dropped the phone and looked again at the shoes. So pretty. And so small to hold such painful memories.

Memories that had never faded despite being locked away for nearly... she had to think... more than twenty-three years. She felt herself drifting back into that fugue state she'd been in and shook her head before getting to her feet. With the shoes in her hands, she climbed the stairs and went to the spare bedroom. Narrow built-in wardrobes with cupboards overhead were set into alcoves either side of a chimney breast. They provided valuable storage but access to the top shelves in the cupboards was hampered by their height. As a result, she used the space for things she rarely needed or things she wanted to remain hidden.

She left the shoes on the undressed bed and dragged a chair through from her bedroom to stand on. It had been a while since she'd opened the top cupboard, and she was surprised to find the box closer than she remembered. She pulled it out and climbed down.

It had originally contained perfume and moisturiser given to her mother one Christmas. Jodie had begged for the pretty box and had kept cinema tickets, photographs, and various other memorabilia in it for years. Before she'd left for Dubai, she'd burned the lot. Apart from one thing.

She sat on the bed with the box on her knee but it was several minutes before she could brace herself to lift the lid. There it was, wrapped in white tissue paper that had discoloured with the passing of time. Reaching in, Jodie gently folded the paper back to reveal the two small blue shoes.

These were knitted ones, blue ribbons laced through and tied in a bow at the front. They were possibly smaller than the ones that had arrived today. She picked them up carefully as if afraid they would disintegrate under her touch and held them to her face, smelling them as if in the hopes they'd have a scent of her child. Not that they could have, she'd never been permitted to see him, touch him, certainly never been able to put the little shoes on his tiny, tiny feet.

A deep sense of longing swept over her, as it always did in the rare times she allowed herself to think of the child she'd had when still a child herself. Giving him up had been the best thing to do. Her mother had convinced her of that then, she was still convinced of it now. It had given him the best chance in life. She had to believe that.

She put both pairs of shoes into the box and took it with her as she went back to the kitchen. Her friend would arrive soon. A smile quivered. Rivka thought she was coming to discuss her career disaster, little did she know it had been put into second place of the things she had to worry about.

Because the person who had left the baby shoes, had to be the person who had given her the first ones.

Victor Hill.

The man Jodie had helped put in prison.

14

Jodie almost smiled at the look of shock on Rivka's face when she put the open box in front of her. 'This pair–' her fingers brushed over the blue ribbon of the older pair '– were the ones Victor gave me when I told him I was pregnant. The other pair came this morning.' She pushed the box gently. 'You can touch them, they won't bite.'

'That doesn't make them any less dangerous.' Rivka moved the box away and looked at Jodie with a worried crease between her eyes. 'You think Victor left them? You should go to the police. Isn't this stalking or something?'

'I can't see them taking the leaving of a pretty gift on my doorknob as being any kind of threat,' Jodie said with an attempt at humour. She reached for the lid of the box and shut the contents away from sight. 'I haven't seen or heard from Victor since the day he was sentenced.'

'But you must have been notified when he was released?'

'I didn't have any direct contact with the family liaison officer that was assigned to us, it all went through Mum. I've no doubt she was told when he was released but she'd never have told me.' Jodie smoothed her hands over the lid of the box. 'She never mentioned what happened again, you know, not in all the years.'

Rivka popped the last piece of a chocolate éclair into her mouth. 'I should have bought two each,' she said, running a finger over the chocolate that stained the plate. She licked it off, then stood to rinse her sticky fingers under the tap. 'Wasn't there anything among her papers about it?'

'There was a writing desk in the living room of our house, an ugly piece of furniture with every drawer crammed with old bills, tax forms and bank statements going back decades.' Her eyes softened at the memory. 'Honestly, everything was shoved into it.' She stayed lost in time for a moment, then felt Rivka's eyes on her pulling her back. 'After she died, when I had to sort out everything, I discovered the desk was almost empty. Mum had known she was dying and destroyed everything apart from her will and information about investments.' Jodie pushed her empty plate away and picked up her tea. 'I know there had been files of documents relating to Victor's arrest and prosecution; I'd seen them when I was looking for a postage stamp one day but I didn't want to look at them and left them untouched. I suppose Mum thought it was best to get rid of it all.'

'So, you've no idea where he is?'

Jodie shook her head slowly. 'No, but he won't be hard to find. He was put on the sex offenders register for life.'

Rivka sat back with a groan. 'You should go to the police, not go looking for him yourself!'

'I didn't say I was going to look for him–'

'You said, *won't,* not wouldn't. That implies you're going to go poking around.'

'Not poking around precisely,' Jodie admitted. 'I can contact the family liaison who was involved in my case or if she's retired, which is quite likely, whoever has taken over her workload and ask where he is.'

'And they'll tell you just like that?' Rivka looked dubious.

Jodie shrugged. She wasn't too sure what her rights were. But if she couldn't find him that way, she'd find him another. 'I can ask, no harm in that. Anyway, let's talk about more cheerful things, like my being fired.' Her grin was forced but it raised a sympathetic smile on her friend's face.

It didn't take long to give Rivka all the details. There weren't many to give.

'It's a crazy situation but at least you're able to get another job.'

'I can apply for one anyway.' Jodie stood and refilled the kettle. She wasn't sure how much coffee or tea she'd drunk that day, but she needed more. She made a fresh pot of tea, emptied the dregs from their mugs and refilled them. 'I suppose I'm lucky, each of the homes I checked out have at least one vacancy.'

'You might end up being better off.'

Jodie reached over and grasped her friend's hand. 'I'm so glad you came over today. Your glass-half-full approach is what I needed to help me cope with all this NMC stuff. And it was good too, to talk about the baby shoes with someone who understands.

'I could stay over, if you like, Tasha wouldn't mind.'

Jodie tried to imagine Tasha's face if Rivka said she was abandoning her to spend the night with her friend. It would widen the streak of jealousy that Jodie had already noted in the younger woman. 'Thanks,' she said, 'but actually I'll have company.' She waited for the penny to drop and laughed at Rivka's look of surprise. 'I met a guy. Flynn. He's...' Jodie tried to think of the right word and shook her head. 'He's special. Sweet and supportive. He insisted on staying here when he heard what I was going through, said he was going to keep staying until I was okay.'

74

Although Rivka tried to look delighted, Jodie could see the worry that appeared in her friend's eyes and wasn't surprised at her hesitant, 'You're not moving too quickly are you? How long have you known him?'

'I know, I know,' Jodie said with a shake of her head. She wasn't normally so spontaneous, it was no wonder Rivka was surprised. 'Less than two weeks, but I feel as though I've known him forever. You'll like him, honestly. And even if nothing long-term comes out of it, it has been so amazing to have him with me on this.' She reached for her mobile. 'Look, he sent me a text earlier to check I was okay.'

Sorry, I didn't get a chance to ring, it's been manic but I've been thinking about you and look forward to hearing all about what happened with your rep later.

Rivka read it and pursed her lips. 'Fine, well if he helps get you through this shitty period that's something I suppose.' She didn't look convinced and dropped her eyes to her twisting fingers before she continued. 'Are you going to tell him about the other business?'

Jodie's eyes flicked to the box. She'd no idea why, after all these years, Victor would choose to send her such a reminder or what he expected to achieve. 'No,' she said quietly. 'Flynn wouldn't understand.'

'You did nothing wrong,' Rivka said, leaning across to take hold of Jodie's hand. 'You've always been too hard on yourself for something you had no control over.'

Jodie felt the warmth of the hand holding hers. She'd never wanted to tell her secret, but a weak moment combined with an excess of alcohol had lowered her defences and she'd spilled her sad tale to a group of nursing friends. They'd been understanding and supportive. The four of them were still friends but only Rivka lived close enough to meet up on a regular basis. 'There'll always be a little part of me that thinks perhaps I led him–'

'Stop right there,' Rivka said, squeezing Jodie's hand. 'You'd just turned fourteen, for goodness' sake, you were a child. Victor was twenty-eight. An adult.' Her face contorted in lines of disgust. 'A rapist.'

Jodie nodded. It was easier. Rivka thought she understood but she didn't... not really. 'I won't tell Flynn, not yet anyway, maybe someday.' She shrugged. 'I think a girlfriend who was fired for gross misconduct is enough for him to take on.'

'That will be cleared up. I'm convinced of it. It'll probably turn out to be that night nurse trying to cause trouble.'

Bessie Abbott? Jodie hadn't given her much thought but it was she who had found the tablets after all. They'd had a good professional rapport, or at least Jodie had thought so, but maybe there was something nasty lurking beneath Bessie's genial exterior.

'We may never know. Taylor said it wasn't his role to find out who left the tablets there, just to ensure I wasn't held responsible for something I swore I didn't do.'

'So, the wrongdoer might get away scot-free?' Rivka sat back and folded her arms. 'That doesn't seem right or fair.'

'No, it doesn't, but I can't worry about that. I have enough on my plate between the medication issue and that package tied to my doorknob. It's almost as if the fates were conspiring against me.' She saw an alert expression on her friend's face. 'What is it?'

'Maybe not the fates,' Rivka said quietly. She unfolded her arms and leaned forward, her lips pressed in a tight line. 'How difficult would it be for someone to gain access to that resident's room in the nursing home and leave those tablets where they would be found?'

Jodie rubbed a hand over her mouth. *How easy would it be?* 'Visitors have to sign in.'

'And does someone check that they are who they say they are?'

Jodie had been in reception on occasion and observed people she'd never seen before walk through the home's open door. They'd sign the book that was left helpfully on the countertop and carry on inside. It never occurred to her to question who they were and, if they didn't know the code for the internal keypad that opened the door between reception and the nursing floor, the receptionist would call it out without questioning their right of entry. 'No, nobody checks. If they looked respectable, it would be assumed that they were visiting someone.'

'Okay,' Rivka said, excitement lighting her eyes. 'Then someone could simply walk in, go into that room, and leave a container of medication, couldn't they?'

Of course they could. Jodie had weighed up the likelihood of one of her colleagues bearing a grudge against her, she'd not thought of an outsider. She locked eyes with Rivka, a grim certainty creeping over her. 'Victor?'

Rivka tilted her chin towards the box. 'The shoes, he used them like a calling card. Even if you hadn't kept them, you were hardly going to forget that he'd given you a pair all those years ago. And coming so soon after that catastrophe in work – it's too much of a coincidence, Jodie. Maybe he is trying to destroy your career, and he wants you to know it's him.'

15

Jodie was exhausted from the mental strain of trying to put it all together by the time Rivka looked at her watch and said she had to go.

'Are you sure you wouldn't like me to stay? I know you have this Flynn fellow coming, but if you're not going to tell him about Victor it means you have to bottle that part of your problems up. Maybe you should–'

Jodie held up a hand to stop her friend. 'No, I'm not going to tell him. Honestly, it will be a relief not to have to keep talking about it.' She saw a quick look of hurt cross Rivka's face. 'I didn't mean that to sound the way it did, I'm sorry. I meant what I said, it helped to be able to talk about it with you.'

Rivka stood and pulled on her raincoat. 'I'm at the end of the phone if you need me. Try to get some rest over the weekend. You look exhausted.' She bent to kiss Jodie gently on the cheek. 'Enjoy this new man in your life. If he makes you happy, he's okay with me.'

'I'll walk to the train station with you,' Jodie said, getting to her feet. 'I was heading out to the shops earlier when I found that package. I was going to cook something, that isn't going to happen now.'

'That's what takeaways were invented for.'

Jodie smiled. 'Very true.'

It wasn't a long walk to the train station and less than ten minutes after leaving home, Jodie was saying goodbye to her friend. 'I'll talk to you over the weekend,' she said, giving her a hug. 'And thanks again, so much, for coming. You're a lifesaver.'

'Remember, if you need me, I'm here for you. Tasha won't mind if you want me to come and stay for a few days.'

Love was definitely blind. Tasha would mind a lot. In fact, she'd probably be furious. Jodie gave her friend's arm a squeeze. 'Thank you, but honestly I'll be fine.'

'Okay, but ring if you need to.' Rivka gave a wave and headed into the station.

Jodie stopped at a local shop. She wasn't going to cook but she still needed some food in the house. Bread, milk, beer, and wine. The necessary staples of life. There were a few takeaways in Gravesend. She'd find out what Flynn liked when he arrived and order something.

She'd turned the corner into Wilfred Street, her house in view, when anxiety hit her and set her heart thumping. Victor knew where she lived. She peered down the short road. It seemed quiet. But maybe he was hiding behind one of the parked cars, waiting to jump out on her.

She'd not been afraid of him when she was fourteen. Looking back from the vantage point of maturity she saw what a wonderful job he'd done in persuading her to trust him, to believe he was god-like, to fall in love with him. That she had done so was something she'd never shared with Rivka who would have argued that she'd been a child, incapable of love. Jodie knew Victor had groomed her and he'd done a good job... but she knew what she'd felt for him had been love. Recognising that it had been wrong, that she had been too young, didn't change that basic truth.

But she wasn't fourteen anymore and if they were right, if Victor had deliberately set out to destroy her career by planting those tablets, he wasn't the man she remembered, the charming Adonis, he was the rapist who had taken advantage of a vulnerable child. Now, for some reason, he'd come looking for her – it was sensible to be afraid.

Lengthening her stride, she hurried along Wilfred Street, taking her keys out as she walked, slipping them into the lock and taking a quick look around before pushing the door open.

How had he found out where she lived? Dumping the shopping bag in the kitchen, she went into the sitting room and pulled the curtains. Had he been peering in her windows, straining to see through the voile she thought had been a sufficient barrier to prying eyes? Maybe venetian blinds or shutters would have been a better option.

She turned, feeling suddenly claustrophobic and hurried from the room to the brighter, airier kitchen. When her life returned to normal, she'd see about getting some shutters; now though, her priority was finding out where Victor was living. She checked the time and frowned. It was almost six. Too late to open that particular can of worms today. Anyway, perhaps it was something best done in person. She remembered the family liaison officer well, her name immediately coming to mind even after all these years of trying to forget. Emma Carlton. In Jodie's memory, she'd been an old woman but to a fourteen-year-old, anyone over thirty was ancient. It was possible she'd only been in her twenties so she might still be working in some capacity. On Monday, Jodie would head to West Hampstead Police Station and find out.

Her anxiety had faded but she was restless and wished Flynn would get there. To keep herself busy, she unpacked the shopping and put the beer and wine in the fridge to chill. Looking around for something else to do, it crossed her mind that she should make some room for Flynn's clothes. His holdall was sitting on the floor in the bedroom: if he were staying for a couple of days, his clothes couldn't remain rolled up inside.

She lifted it onto the bed. Wouldn't it be nice to surprise him by unpacking, maybe ironing shirts if there were more inside and making room in the drawers for his things? He'd been so kind to come and spend time with her and it wasn't as if she were rewarding him with earth-shattering sex.

The thought brought a smile to her lips. Humming, she squashed the contents of the top drawer of her chest of drawers into the one below, then turned to unpack the holdall. It was tightly packed, the contents bouncing upward as soon as the zip was opened and spilling dark socks onto the bed. She picked them up and put them into the drawer, then quickly unpacked the rest. Boxer shorts, a couple of T-shirts and a pair of jeans were all folded neatly away. The two white shirts on the bottom she slipped onto hangers, frowning at the creases. It would only take a minute to run an iron over them. She kept her iron and ironing board in the spare bedroom and she was soon at work, the steam iron smoothing out every line. It would be nice if she could do the same with her life.

A few minutes later, she hung them in the space she'd made in the wardrobe, running her hands along the sleeves. She didn't recognise the make but she knew quality when she saw and felt it, and these were quality. Flynn was a man with expensive taste. He was probably more used to going out with glamorous, successful women. Not a woman who'd been fired or who was being stalked by a rapist. That she'd done nothing wrong in either case didn't make her situation easier to accept or make it all any the less frustrating.

She closed the wardrobe door and, satisfied that the holdall was empty, she zipped it shut and pushed it under the bed.

The ring of the doorbell brought her head up with a jerk. Flynn!

Her feet barely touched the ground as she dashed down the stairs and grabbed the doorknob, grinning in excitement. But before she could twist the knob to open the door, the grin faded, replaced by a sad smile of self-awareness. She was looking on Flynn as her saviour. What a burden to put on him, to put on their relationship. She needed to get a grip.

The doorbell rang again.

Jodie took a calming breath, turned the knob, and pulled the door open. 'Hi.'

'Hi, so sorry I didn't have a chance to ring earlier,' Flynn said, stepping inside and planting a kiss on her lips. 'It's been one of those days.' He lifted a plastic carrier bag. 'I stopped and got a bottle of wine, thought you might be in need of a glass or two.'

'Or three or four.' She laughed, taking the bag and heading into the kitchen. 'I bought wine and beer too. I had planned to cook dinner but the idea faded pretty quickly. I thought we might get a takeaway.'

'Suits me fine.' He took his jacket off and loosened his tie. 'Right, tell me how it went.'

Jodie opened the red wine he'd brought and poured them both a glass. 'Sit, I'll tell you everything, not that there's much to tell.' When she'd finished, she sat back and took a gulp of her wine. 'My friend Rivka came around this afternoon.' Jodie took another drink of her wine before she continued, keeping her eyes fixed on her glass as she told him an edited version of what her friend had said. 'She suggested that it was a random stranger who came into the home and left the tablets there to cause trouble.'

'But why?' Flynn lifted his hands. 'No, don't answer that, why does any idiot do the things they do? Maybe it was someone with a grudge against the home and you happened to get caught up in it.'

'It's as good a reason as any.'

'You're going to put that theory to your union rep?'

'Yes, I will. Anything that will shake the home's certainty that I was to blame will help my case. But it's going to be months before it's all sorted.'

'I'll be here to help you through it. And at least you can work.' Flynn picked up the bottle, filled their glasses and reached his free hand out to caress her cheek. 'You're sure that's all it is? You look sad tonight.'

It was the perfect opportunity to tell him about the baby shoes, about Victor. About the baby she'd had and given away. Instead, she lay a hand over his. 'I'm a little tired, that's all. And maybe a little worried about it all.'

'You'll find it easy to get another position, won't you? Nurses are always sought after, especially experienced ones like you.'

Jodie smiled at his certainty. 'I've sent off my CV to the other homes in the area. I'm hopeful.' Her expression turned serious. 'I could always go back to work in operating theatres or try something else entirely. Maybe I'll have a think.'

In fact, an idea had come to her as she was unpacking Flynn's bag. All his expensive clothes. Sales representatives earned incredibly good money. She knew a few nurses who'd taken the plunge and all were doing well. Perhaps it was something she should think about.

For the moment, she'd keep her idea to herself. She didn't want to be swayed by Flynn or anyone else, one way or another.

16

They ordered a Chinese takeaway from a restaurant Jodie liked and sat eating at the small table overlooking the courtyard garden. Solar lights that Jodie had spent a fortune on came on and added an extra magic touch to their evening.

'This is very pretty,' Flynn said, manipulating his chopsticks with a skill Jodie, who'd thought she did well, envied. 'You've managed to do a lot with a small space.'

'Thank you, I'm very lucky.' And she was, she realised. Sitting there in her lovely home, with a gorgeous man. 'Tell me about your job? What made you decide to become a sales representative?'

Flynn put his chopsticks down and pushed his plate away. 'That was really good,' he said, picking up his beer glass. 'Why did I decide to become a sales rep? Well, it's not an overly exciting story. When I finished my BA in university, I dossed around before somebody suggested I should apply for a sales job.' He grinned. 'It seems I have the gift of the gab. So, I applied.' He held up his hands. 'And that was that.'

'And you've never regretted it?'

He shook his head. 'Why would I? It pays well. I get to meet a wide range of interesting people, get to travel to sales conferences and such, where I stay in nice hotels. It's a good job.' He stopped and looked at her through suddenly narrowed eyes. 'Why? Are you thinking you might like it?'

She hoped her laugh didn't sound forced. 'No, I like what I do. I'm simply curious.'

'Good,' he said firmly, 'because whereas I like it, it's a tough job. I have rhinoceros-like skin, you'd be gobbled up and spat out in no time.'

Jodie looked down at the table so he wouldn't see the annoyance that flickered in her eyes. He'd been so kind, so supportive over this whole mess she'd gotten herself into. Did it matter that he seemed to see her as a weak pushover when she was anything but? Was that what being fired had resulted in... a shrinking of her role as a professional experienced nurse, a lessening of her power, her place?

Flynn reached for the bottle and topped up their glasses again. He wasn't even aware he'd annoyed her. Perhaps she was taking it too personally. He was, after all, trying to be kind. To protect her. There was nothing wrong with that.

The weekend passed in a haze of long walks and cosy lunches in local pubs. In the evenings, they relaxed in front of the TV, ordering takeaways, enjoying their favourite programmes, delighted to find they had similar taste.

Jodie shied away from talking about her predicament, giving monosyllabic answers when Flynn brought the topic up, until he finally turned to look at her with one eyebrow raised. 'You don't want to discuss it?'

They were walking hand in hand along Gordon Promenade enjoying a lazy Sunday afternoon. Jodie was pretending everything was right in her world. She didn't want to talk about being fired. It might have been good to talk about Victor, to use Flynn as a sounding board for some of the crazy ideas that raced through her head. But that would entail telling Flynn about her past and she wasn't willing to do that and to see his expression change to one of pity. She tightened her fingers around his. 'This investigation will take three or four months according to my rep. I want to try to forget about it as much as I can.' She stopped and turned to face him, the breeze blowing her hair in a whirl around her head. She held it back with one hand. 'I don't want every conversation to be about me, Flynn. It makes me seem so...' She sought for the right word but he pulled her closer with the hand he held and wrapped his other arm around her.

'There's nothing wrong with being needy,' he said into her ear. 'I quite like being your knight in shining armour.'

It wasn't the word she was looking for at all. *Needy,* was that how he viewed her? She was horrified at the thought and wanted to argue the point, wanted to say she'd meant self-obsessed or even self-centred, but not *needy*. What a horrible word that was. But as he continued to hold her in the warmth of his arms as the chilly breeze swirled around them, she decided it didn't matter.

It wasn't until much later – when Flynn was breathing heavily beside her and she was lying, eyes wide-open, a slight smile of sexual satisfaction curving her lips, her brain in a post-coital torpor – that a tiny voice worked its way into her ear. He hadn't mentioned either going home or staying with her longer.

She sat up a little to look at him. He was sleeping prone, his face turned towards her, one arm curved under his head, the other hanging over the side of the bed. The curtains weren't closed properly and light leaked through from the street lights outside, casting an eerie glow over his almost too-perfect features.

Too perfect. The words rattled in her brain and dampened the sense of euphoria she'd been wallowing in for the last hour. It was so perfect it scared her.

She flopped back and rested her hand across her eyes to shut out the light. What were the odds of the ideal relationship coming when her life was in such a turmoil? The gods, she decided, were having a laugh at her expense.

Sleep wasn't coming. She slipped from the bed, pulled on a robe, and tiptoed down the stairs. The curtains were still shut in the sitting room, but before Jodie switched on the light, she checked there was no gap for anyone to peer through. A safety measure, she told herself. She wasn't getting paranoid because Victor knew where she lived, because he'd left her a totally inappropriate gift... no, not a gift. A reminder.

That last came out of the blue, blindsiding her and making her drop heavily onto the sofa, a hand over her mouth to soften the gasp of fear. Was that what those sweet blue baby shoes were supposed to do? To remind her of the future they had planned together, the two of them and their baby, a future that had been yanked from under their feet when her mother had noticed her swelling belly.

She'd never spoken to Victor again; never been allowed to, and when the child was gone, when it was all over and she was in a different place, a different school, it was put into her past and locked down.

The next day, she'd find him and see why, after all these years, he'd decided to reappear. With no sign of the sleep she needed, Jodie reached under the sofa for her laptop and stretched to switch on a table lamp. In the circle of light, she started to prepare for the following day.

Despite what Flynn had said, the idea of looking for a position as a sales rep hadn't gone away. She did an internet search for some nursing recruitment agencies, fascinated by the array of jobs that were available. And the amount of positions in sales.

There were a number that appealed. They gave little details, merely asking for a CV to be sent for their consideration. Within thirty minutes, Jodie had sent hers to three different recruitment agencies. Surely, one of them might come through for her.

She shut the laptop, slipped it underneath the sofa then tucked her legs under her robe and curled up. If she couldn't sleep, she could at least rest. But it seemed as if making plans of any sort eased her spinning mind and she drifted into a light sleep filled with strange dreams, none of which she could remember when her eyes opened sometime later.

It was the squeak of floorboards that had disturbed her. It must be seven, the same time Flynn had rolled from bed the previous Thursday and Friday. Jodie missed the absolute quiet of living on her own, she wasn't ready yet to cohabit, certainly not with a boyfriend of less than two weeks – perfect though he might be. Maybe over breakfast, she might suggest it was time he went home. The catastrophic shock of being fired had eased. It was time to grab onto some semblance of normality.

But the opportunity for discussion didn't come. Twenty minutes later she heard hurried steps on the stairs and the door jerked open to show Flynn still in the act of tying his tie, harried lines creasing his brow. 'I'm late,' he said, 'have to dash. See you later.' He crossed to her side, bent, and brushed his lips against her cheeks. With a final wave, he rushed out the door.

Jodie hadn't had a chance to say a word and was still struggling to get to her feet when she heard the front door slam shut. Puzzled, she picked up her phone, her eyes widening when she saw the time. Not seven thirty as she'd thought, but eight thirty. He was leaving much later than usual. She hoped he didn't have an important meeting lined up. Her fingers flew over the phone keys.

I hope you catch up with your day, xx

The text sent, she lay back and shut her eyes. She'd have a talk with him that night. He'd probably be relieved to get back to his swish city apartment.

Her plans for that morning pushed her work problems and Flynn from her head. Now instead of his handsome face, Victor's was there, as it had been all those years before, handsome, charming, and utterly compelling. She wondered what sort of man he'd grown into.

Less than an hour later, wearing her smartest jeans, white T-shirt, and pale-blue linen jacket, her damp hair pinned up in a tight knot, she was ready to go. A constant churning in her stomach made her decide against breakfast. She'd get a takeaway coffee in the station and have it on the train.

Gravesend station was a bustling, heaving mass of commuters arriving, leaving, standing about getting in the way. Jodie, with her priorities right, bought her coffee before heading to the automatic ticket machines for a return ticket to West Hampstead and hurried to the platform with minutes to spare before the Southeastern train pulled out.

She was in luck and managed to find a seat. As the train chugged along, her thoughts drifted back to a period of her life that was fraught with conflicting emotions of love and hate. She had been convinced she'd loved Victor. Her mother, the social worker and even the prosecuting team had told her she was too young to understand, that she was a child. She'd cupped her hands around her baby bump and argued that she loved him... that she was old enough to know what she wanted.

She smiled at her naivety. She'd been just a child, a confused and very young fourteen-year-old desperately trying to replace the father who had died so suddenly the year before. The ideal vulnerable candidate for a manipulative man like Victor.

The train pulled into St Pancras International and she shuffled off behind a line of commuters. A few minutes later she was on Platform 1 waiting for the Thameslink train to her destination, sipping the last of her cold coffee. There were others on the platform; a young woman with a small child held tightly by the hand, an older couple looking bored, and a few men travelling alone. She stared at each intently wondering if any of them was Victor. They were all around the right age and her eyes narrowed as she inspected their features, looking for any reminder of the man she'd once adored. But there was nothing. One of the men caught her eye and leered. She looked quickly away.

There was no sense of familiarity as she walked through the doors of West Hampstead Police Station. Too many years had passed. It didn't matter, Jodie knew why she was there and what she wanted. She wanted assurances from the family liaison, be that Emma Carlton or her successor, that Victor was no threat to her. Jodie wanted them to arrange a meeting with him where she could discuss their shared unfortunate past and lay to bed any worries that he was implicated in her trouble at work. Maybe he'd confess to leaving the baby shoes for some strange reason of his own. He'd apologise, promise to leave her alone, and that would be that.

That was what she wanted.

What she got was shockingly different.

17

Emma Carlton had been a relatively inexperienced twenty-six-year-old when she'd been appointed family liaison for the Armstrongs. Almost thirty years in the service had changed her physically and mentally. Several years before, when her drinking had given her cause for concern, she'd successfully broken the bad habit of using alcohol to combat stress and had taken up running. As with her drinking, she took it to excess and as a result her physique was wiry, her face gaunt and her skin wrinkled from too many hours in the sun.

Running had allowed her to cope with the stress of her job, but the cause of it remained. The endless stories of sorrow and suffering, the terrible pain that one person had inflicted on another, sometimes simply because they could... they all gnawed away at the part of her that had once believed in the basic decency of people. Now, there was little of that faith in people left.

She'd been promoted to manager a few years before. It had reduced the stress a little; nowadays she spent more of her time in the office than out in the field. Reading the reports rather than hearing them, however, didn't diminish their power to disturb.

It had been a few years since she'd accepted a new case but she continued to manage her older ones, few of which required more than the occasional meeting to discuss a perpetrator's release. She was used to parole officers, the police and various other disciplines contacting her for information regarding certain cases, but it was rare for a victim to turn up after so many years to seek the same.

'You want to know where Victor Hill is currently living?' Emma had met all sorts in her career. The rather garbled, and certainly tangled account of medication errors and baby shoes made her look at Jodie with carefully assessing eyes. Sometimes a normal exterior, like the one she was portraying so well, was a cover for a twisted interior.

'I know you're probably unable to give me his address,' Jodie was saying. 'I wouldn't want to meet him on my own anyway. What I was hoping is that you could instigate a meeting between us so that I could discuss what I've told you.'

Emma's hands were clasped on the table in front of her. She tapped her thumbs together as she thought about what the woman had said. 'You think that Victor is responsible for planting the medication that got you fired, following it up by leaving the baby shoes tied to your door so you'd know exactly who was responsible.'

When Jodie nodded, Emma stopped tapping and spread her hands. 'Why? And why baby shoes? Why not a note saying what he'd done?'

Jodie had asked herself the same question. She looked at the stony face of the woman opposite, remembering her as being more supportive, kinder. Maybe it was easier to be kind to a fourteen-year-old.

Jodie folded her arms, gripping her biceps tightly. 'I'm not sure. Maybe he saw my comfortable life and wanted to unsettle it by getting me into trouble at work. He may not have been aware of the seriousness of what he did. Leaving the shoes...' The memories came slipping back again, the young Jodie so much in thrall to the older man, her eyes shining when she opened the gift he'd bought her, the blue baby shoes wrapped so carefully, chosen with love. She'd told everyone about them at the time – her mother, the legal team, the police – wanting them to see that Victor wasn't the monster they were portraying. 'He would have known I'd remember them. Before everything came out, we'd planned to have the baby together. We'd even spoken about running away.'

'I remember,' Emma said. 'You couldn't see any fault with him. Even when other victims came forward to claim he'd molested them, you refused to see it.'

'Yet it was my testimony that put him away.' Jodie remembered the kindly judge sitting down with her and asking her to tell her everything, the subtle nudging questions when she'd been reluctant to go into details about the increasing sexualisation of her relationship with Victor, culminating in what she'd remembered as being the less-than-pleasant experience of sex on the rough ground behind shrubs and trees on the Heath. Not painful, Victor had made sure of that, but not particularly nice.

'You did the right thing,' Emma insisted.

Had she? She'd been so conflicted then, a confused, frightened child. Now, she might be confused... even a little frightened... but she wasn't conflicted. 'Anyway, all that is irrelevant,' Jodie said bluntly. 'Are you able to arrange a meeting with him, or not?'

'Not, I'm afraid.' The words may have been apologetic but the tone of voice wasn't.

'Fine.' Jodie got to her feet. 'It's no problem. He's on the sex offenders list, no doubt I can get access to that somewhere. Thanks for your time.'

Emma shook her head. 'Sit down, you don't understand.'

Jodie sat and folded her arms again. 'Don't tell me he's dead because I don't believe it.'

'As far as I know, he's still alive and well.'

'As far as you know?' Jodie gave an uncertain laugh.

'The general public–' Emma pointed a finger at Jodie to encompass her in this collective '–think that being put on the register of sex offenders for life means that. Well, I hate to break the bad news to you but it means life in much the same way as someone who is sentenced to life in prison.'

'What?' Shock caused Jodie's mouth to drop open. She shut it with an audible snap. 'That can't be right.'

'It may not be right, but it is the law. After fifteen years on the register an offender can apply to have his name removed.' Emma lifted both hands, palms upward and fingers splayed as if to say it was all out of her hands. 'They simply need to prove they are no longer a risk to the public.' She pulled the keypad of her desktop computer nearer and tapped a few keys. 'I have an excellent memory for names so I remember seeing his application was granted. My memory for dates isn't quite so good.' She looked at the screen then back to Jodie. 'Victor Hill was removed from the register four weeks ago.'

Shock kept Jodie silent, her eyes blinking in confusion. Her brain, processing, latched onto one point. 'If he could have had his name removed years ago, why did he wait so long?'

Emma tapped a few more keys and shook her head. 'He did apply, more than once in fact, but it wasn't until this application that they were convinced he proved no risk to the public. He had, it appears, attended a clinic which purports to treat sexual deviancy.'

Jodie stared at her in disbelief. 'Seriously?'

'According to the reports, this particular clinic works on the basis that sexual deviancy is an illness and as such can respond to treatment. Victor spent a month there following which he reapplied to have his name removed. This time the application was granted.'

'He's no longer considered a threat?'

'No.' Emma looked back to the screen and frowned. 'It seems a letter sent to him came back as undelivered so it looks as if he's moved from where he was too.'

'So, he no longer has to inform the police where he is living... and he is no longer forced by law to keep his distance from his victims... from me.' Jodie saw the confirmation in Emma's suddenly kinder expression. 'I suppose, I don't have to wonder anymore why I'm hearing from him now, do I?'

18

All Emma Carlton could do was advise Jodie to report the baby shoes to the police. 'As for your theory that he may have planted the medication to incriminate you–' she shrugged '–I think you'd have a hard job proving that.'

Jodie got to her feet and extended her hand. 'Thank you for your help and for being kind to me all those years ago, I'm not sure I ever did thank you then.'

A smile transformed Emma's face and Jodie saw the woman she was before life had left its mark. 'Actually,' Emma said, 'you thanked me a number of times. You were a sweet child. You were also unbelievably malleable, it was easy to see why Hill had chosen you.' She stood, took Jodie's hand, and held it in a firm grip. 'I wondered what would become of you. It looks to me as though you've turned out very well. Take my advice and don't let... whatever this is, ruin that.'

Whatever this is. That was the problem. Jodie had no idea and her hope that she'd get some answers here had been swept away. But life had also left its mark on Jodie; she may have been a biddable girl but she'd developed a core of steel since then.

'No, I won't,' she said and with that, she turned and left the office.

She'd no intention of taking Emma's advice to report the baby shoes to the police. Even if she went into detail about her past, about the baby shoes mirroring the shoes Victor had given her all those years before, she couldn't see them taking any action against him. Leaving a gift hanging from her doorknob would hardly be classified as a threatening act.

Emma had been correct too, Jodie would have had an impossible job convincing the police that Victor was involved in planting the medication. She'd no proof apart from a gut feeling and although she knew gut feelings were beloved of crime writers she guessed, in real life, they would tend to rely more on facts.

Her hands shoved into her jacket pocket, she retraced her steps to West Hampstead train station and caught the next available train back to St Pancras International. Instead of changing platforms to catch the train to Gravesend she exited the station and crossed the busy road, joining the crowd that weaved in and out of Kings Cross station. It was one of her favourite places, always bustling, always bright and it was comforting to blend in with the hordes of people who travelled through. As she walked, her thoughts tumbled in a crazy tangle. Nothing made sense. She needed to talk it over with someone who had a cool head in a crisis. Rivka. The choice was automatic as it always was.

It was almost midday. The clinic where Rivka worked was shut for lunch for an hour at twelve thirty, if she hurried, Jodie might be able to grab her for a chat. Talking about everything might make things clearer in her head. Her thoughts switched to Flynn. Maybe someday, he would be her first choice but it was too soon in their relationship. So far, their conversations had been mostly superficial, touching on what they liked to do, eat and drink, not on who they were, certainly not on who they'd been in the past.

It wasn't until she was on the Piccadilly Line that she realised that she was still searching every man's face for a resemblance to Victor Hill. He knew where she lived, and where she worked. What else did he know about her? He could be any of the men who was strolling by. Her memories of him were distorted not simply by time but by the childish infatuation that had made him appear like a god. Any ordinary-looking man of a certain age could be him.

The thought made her tense and she anxiously looked around the carriage, relieved when minutes later the train reached its first stop, her destination, Holloway Road station. It was only a five-minute walk from there to the private clinic.

A receptionist Jodie knew to see, greeted her with a friendly nod. 'Hi Jodie, is Rivka expecting you?'

'No, but I was hoping to catch her for a chat.'

Some of the anxiety and stress of the morning must have shown on Jodie's face and the receptionist's smile was replaced by a look of concern. 'You look like you've had a bad morning, take a seat, I'll see if I can find her for you.'

Jodie wasn't waiting long, her friend bursting through to reception with a grin on her face and words of greeting on her lips. 'You should have rung, we could have gone out somewhere.' She took the seat beside Jodie. 'You look so sad, what's happened?'

'Not sad, at least not really. More downright mad.' Jodie filled her in on the morning's meeting.

Rivka's eyes grew wider as she listened. 'Bloody hell. I thought once you were on the register, you were on it for life.'

'It seems that's not the way it works.'

'Then you've no idea where Victor is?'

Jodie shook her head. 'According to Emma Carlton, as soon

as his name was removed, he left the rented apartment he was living in. He'd no obligation thereafter to inform the authorities where he lived.'

'What about his family? There must be someone you could contact.'

'I was fourteen. I never met any of them, never even saw them. They were at his trial, of course, but don't forget, I gave my evidence behind closed doors so never saw them there either.' She shrugged. 'I have a vague idea there was a sister living in Wales or somewhere.'

'Hill is a pretty common surname.' Rivka tapped her fingers on the side of her chair. 'It wouldn't be easy to track them down.'

'I know.' Jodie sighed loudly. 'His parents may not even be alive and his sister is possibly married so her name could be anything.'

'What are you going to do?'

'I don't know.' She saw Rivka's frown and tilted her head. 'What?'

'I was thinking about the baby shoes.' Rivka's tone was anxious, as if afraid of what she was about to suggest. 'I was just thinking of who else would have reason to remind you of that baby and the answer slapped me in the face.' She leaned forward and put her hand over Jodie's. 'Haven't you considered that it might be your son?'

19

Jodie remembered the tears. The tantrums. The vocal demands. She'd begged and pleaded with her mother to tell her where her son had gone, swore to her that she simply wanted one look before he vanished forever.

One look. She'd never seen him, her mother holding her hands tightly over the sobbing Jodie's eyes when the baby, after one gut-wrenching push, was finally delivered into a world that swirled around his mother, a maelstrom of pain for a fourteen-year-old to cope with. Jodie hadn't seen him then and the long and difficult birth had rendered her incapable of fighting her cause for days. It wasn't until the pain of the birth had faded that Jodie fought to take one look at her son. Fought in vain.

Her mother remained adamant that it was for the best. That it would be easier for her to forget, easier to put the whole terrible ordeal behind her. Finally, she'd grabbed the weeping Jodie by her shoulders and told her bluntly, 'He's gone away. The family that adopted him emigrated as soon as the paperwork was signed.'

It wasn't until years later that Jodie found out that her mother had lied, that the paperwork didn't happen that quickly, but back then she'd believed everything she was told and she'd howled her loss.

'Australia,' her mother had said when Jodie had begged to know where he'd gone and she'd taken some comfort when she'd visited her local library and sat with every book they had on the continent, poring over photographs, imagining the baby growing up among koala bears and kangaroos.

When she was older, she'd had a longer conversation with her mother. About the baby, and the adoption. And Jodie had learned the harrowing truth.

Her eyes filled at the memory. She looked across to Rivka's expectant face. 'No, it wouldn't be him.' Jodie saw the receptionist's curious face and leaned closer. 'You remember my mother?' She laughed when Rivka raised her eyebrow. 'Yes, she wasn't the kind of woman you forgot, was she? Well, she was even tougher than you know. The adoption was private. All legal and above board and everything, but Mum made certain conditions before the final paperwork was signed.'

'But she wasn't the mother, you had to have signed everything,' Rivka argued.

Jodie shrugged. 'My mother was a force of nature. You didn't argue with her. Certainly, I didn't. I signed where I was told, did what I was told.' Her voice faded as she drifted into the past.

Rivka reached out and gave her a shake. 'What did she do?'

Jodie pulled herself back to the present. 'Sorry. There's an Adoption Contacts Register, Rivka. The adopted person or the birth parents can choose to be on it so that if either wants to contact the other, it's possible.' She took a deep breath. 'The register also has another option – you can choose to have an absolute veto allowing no contact whatsoever. My mother signed that veto.'

Rivka's mouth dropped open. 'But you can have that changed, surely? You must have the right.'

Rights, obligations, promises. 'Mum said it was for the best. That it would be better for the child to imagine his beginning rather than know the truth.' Jodie met her friend's sympathetic eyes. 'A child of rape, the son of a sexual predator. How could I wish that on my child? I promised her I'd never change the veto. There's no way the child would be able to find out anything about me.'

'What about the birth certificate?'

'What about it?' She saw confusion cross her friend's face. 'I'm not going to be on it. As soon as the court grants the adoption, a copy of the order is sent to the General Register Office and they enter the details in the Adopted Children's Register. After that, I'm wiped away. A new certificate of birth is issued in the child's new name. There is no reference on it to him being adopted so there's no guarantee that his parents ever even told him. He was a newborn: and they were heading to Australia. It would have been simple to pass him off as their own. Simpler for all concerned.' Jodie smiled. 'And you may bet it was what my mother would have encouraged.'

'Then we're back to it being Victor who left the baby shoes.'

'And back to trying to figure out why.' Jodie rested her head against the wall behind. 'Looks like I'm going to have to wait for whatever he does next.'

'He had his name removed from the sex offenders register only four weeks ago,' Rivka said, her forehead creased as she puzzled a thought through. 'Maybe he had nothing to do with the medication being left in the nursing home and leaving the shoes was a memorial thing or something, marking an end to a period in his life. Perhaps that's all you'll hear from him.'

'Perhaps.' It was only a thread of hope to hang on to but it was something. 'Thanks for listening. It helps to talk about it with someone who knows my history.'

Rivka checked her watch. 'I guess that means you haven't

told lover boy.' She gave Jodie a reassuring smile. 'That's not a criticism. You've plenty of time to tell him if you want to. Now, I'd better get back to work.'

They stood together. Rivka reached for Jodie and enveloped her in a hug. 'I want to hear all about him, next time we meet.'

'Until I get another job, I'll have plenty of time to meet for coffee so lots of time to fill you in. Suffice to say that it's going well. He's gorgeous, you'll like him.'

'Just what you need. Better fly.' And Rivka was gone in a flurry of hand-waving, still waving as she hurried across reception and through a door at the back, leaving Jodie with a smile on her lips that gradually faded as she considered what her friend had suggested. Perhaps she was right. Maybe it was simply Victor's way of marking the end of a chapter.

20

For Victor, having his name removed from the register of sex offenders was supposed to be the start of a new life, one where every sex crime within a fifty-mile radius didn't bring the police to his door. After the first few times, when he truly couldn't remember where he'd been on specific dates which resulted in his being questioned for hours, he'd started to write down where he was every day, an hourly account of his sad, miserable existence that he pulled out for the police's benefit thereafter when they called.

The day his name was removed, he celebrated by going back to his seedy bedsit, packing all his belongings in one large holdall and leaving without giving notice. It meant forfeiting his deposit but it also meant nobody knowing when he'd left or where he'd gone. It was a day he'd longed for. The start of a new life. He carried his holdall to the nearest train station and sat in a concourse café watching commuters stride past with a sense of purpose in every step.

A sense of purpose. Victor had one, although his would probably be called an obsession. He had thought to leave it behind, to erase Jodie from his life much as his name had been from that damn register but as he sat and watched the crowds wafting past, he knew he couldn't do it.

He'd loved her from the first moment he'd seen her at a bus stop. The neat school uniform had caught his eye but it was the tangle of hair escaping from a band to fall higgledy-piggledy around her face that had tugged at his heart. He'd started a conversation and by the time the bus arrived, she was looking at him with admiration and his heart was hers.

As the doors slid open, he'd been desperate not to let her go. 'Can I see you again?'

She'd looked at him with her big blue eyes. 'I get this one home every day.' Then she'd hurried on, sat downstairs, and smiled at him through the window as the bus took off.

And that was it. He'd waited for her the next day and the day after. At the weekends, they'd meet on Hampstead Heath and walk for miles or sit and admire the London skyline and talk about their future. In the wooded nooks and crannies of the park they'd hold hands and it was there, late one summer's evening hidden amongst the trees, that they'd first made love.

It was a precious memory. He'd thought she'd loved him but she'd given him up, had turned on him without a thought, cast away their dreams, their future. He knew her mother had been partially responsible, but Jodie had known him, had known how much he loved her. He'd told them all, the police, solicitors, the judge, that they were wrong, that those other girls had meant nothing to him, that Jodie was the one he loved, the one he'd wanted. He remembered their scornful, hateful looks, their quick use of the word 'rapist' to describe him, a word that had shocked him to the core. That wasn't who he was at all.

21

Back home, following her meeting with Rivka, weariness settled over Jodie and she plodded up the stairs, kicked off her shoes and lay fully clothed on the bed. She shut her eyes and begged sleep to come. It didn't, of course. After almost an hour trying, she groaned, sat up and swung her feet to the floor.

Anyway, she had the pressing matter of finding herself another job. She switched on her laptop in the hope that one of the three homes she'd emailed had replied. Two had, and a flicker of excitement washed away a little of the tiredness. But opening the first, she saw that their only current vacancy was for a night nurse. Nights, she hated them.

The second was more hopeful. They were looking for a part-time day nurse. Twenty-four hours a week with the possibility of more to cover holidays and sick leave. Twenty-four hours. Almost half the hours she'd wanted. But she didn't have a mortgage on the house, her needs were low and she could lower them. It was something she'd have to consider.

There was no reply from the third nursing home but, more interestingly, there was one from one of the recruitment agencies. They'd love to have a chat with her, gave her a contact name and asked her to ring.

Jodie sat staring at the screen for a few seconds. Maybe this was fate taking a hand and this was going to turn out to be the silver lining to that darkly brooding cloud that was hanging over her. She reached for her phone, dialled the number on the screen and asked to speak to Nate Bisby.

'Nate here, how can I help?'

'Hi,' Jodie said nervously. 'It's Jodie Armstrong. I had an email asking me to ring.'

'Jodie! Yes, hello. Thank you for getting back to me so quickly. I read your CV and was impressed with it. Especially–' Jodie heard the faint tap of keys '–your experience in operating theatres. I have an exciting position with a pharmaceutical company, one specialising in anaesthetic drugs. Would that be something that would interest you?'

Would it? Jodie was taken aback. Yes, she guessed it would. 'It sounds interesting,' she said, hoping he wouldn't think her reply lacked enthusiasm. 'Actually, it sounds like exactly what I'm looking for.'

'Great, great. How soon can you come in for a chat?'

Feeling slightly bewildered by the speed this was all happening, Jodie took a deep breath. Maybe this was the wrong idea. Flynn was probably right, she wasn't tough enough for this whirlwind world.

'Just a chat, no commitment. And if you decide it doesn't suit, perhaps there's something else that might.'

What harm could it do to go and speak to him? 'Tomorrow. I could come in tomorrow.'

Agreeing on a time, she put the phone down and laughed in surprised disbelief. She wasn't sure if it was a silver lining or not but maybe getting fired would catapult her into a better life.

She'd been a nurse for almost sixteen years. Maybe it was time to try something else.

Flynn mightn't approve but there was no point in telling him until there was reason to. She was going for a chat and might not be interested when she heard the details. There was also the possibility that they might not be interested when they heard about the NMC investigation. That thought rocked her. Maybe she was wasting her time.

She rested her head back on the sofa. There was no harm in going... it was as good a way as any to fill her day. When her mobile phone rang, she picked it up, saw Flynn's name on the screen and pressed to accept the call. 'Hi.'

'Jodie, hi, sorry for not ringing earlier, it's been a crazy day. Listen, I think I'll stay at my place tonight.'

Earlier, she'd have been pleased to have heard this, now contrarily, she was disappointed. 'Okay.'

'I'm glad you sound disappointed. Miss me, I'll certainly miss you. I'd come over but I have an early meeting tomorrow and I need to be on time.'

'No, that's fine. I'm really tired anyway, going to have an early night.'

'How's the job hunt going?'

It was tempting to tell him about the recruitment agency and maybe she would when they met, face to face. 'I had a reply from two of the homes. One has a vacancy that might be an option.'

'Oh good, that must be a relief. Stuff that other place. That nursing body will soon clear you and everything will be back to normal.'

Normal! She almost laughed. 'Yes, I'm sure it will.'

'How about dinner on Wednesday? I could stay over... if you'd like?'

She'd like very much. 'That sounds like a plan. Hopefully, I'll have more news on the job front by then.'

They chatted a few minutes more, Flynn telling her an amusing story about one of his customers which made her chuckle and wonder, yet again, whether sales wouldn't be the ideal job for her.

~

After yet another restless night, Jodie dragged herself from her bed and thought about cancelling the meeting with the recruitment consultant but the thought of a long day doing nothing was more exhausting. A few mugs of strong coffee and a long cool shower perked her up a little and with the idea that she had nothing to lose by going, she dressed in smarter-than-usual clothes, left the house and walked briskly to the train station.

It was rush hour, the train packed with commuters of all ages but it was the men of a certain age who attracted Jodie's intent gaze. Any one of them could be Victor. In St Pancras International, she stopped and pretended to use her mobile while the commuters swarmed around her, parting and joining again, intent on their destination. Apart from one woman who glared at Jodie for standing in her way, nobody gave her a passing glance. With a shake of her head at her paranoia, she pocketed her phone and walked on.

The recruitment agency was, conveniently, a short walk from St Pancras station and Jodie was outside the office at five minutes to the agreed 10am meeting. With nervous excitement blanketing her worry about Victor, she pushed open the door into a tiny reception area and was immediately directed down a long echoing corridor.

Nate Bisby, a short, plump man with unusually pale skin and

a bad comb-over, greeted her at the door of his office, holding out his hand and taking hers in a firm grip. 'Thank you for coming, come in, sit. Would you like some coffee?' When she shook her head, he waved her to a seat and sat behind his desk.

'We've recruited a number of nurses as sales representatives,' he said, sitting with his hands clasped across his chest. 'Your employment history working in operating theatres would fit perfectly. It's a little unfortunate it was abroad.' He shook his head. 'This business, you see, it's all about contacts, getting your foot in the door. If you'd worked in hospitals here, you'd know people. Anaesthetists,' he added, as if feeling the need to spell it out.

Jodie smiled. 'There was an active social community in Dubai. When I came back to the UK, I joined the Ex-Expats Club and keep in regular contact with some of the people I used to work with. Including–' her smile broadened '–several anaesthetists who work in London hospitals.'

Bisby's face lit up. 'Excellent! That improves your chances dramatically.' He unclasped his hands and tapped his fingers on the desk. 'They're looking for someone to start as soon as possible. How much notice do you need to give in your current position?'

Jodie cleared her throat. 'Actually, I don't need to give any.' She kept her head down as she told her tale, reluctant to see disappointment cross his face. When she finished, she looked up, expecting to hear him offer his regrets that he couldn't continue.

Instead, Bisby shrugged. 'I used to be a nurse,' he said, surprising her. 'I know what the NMC is like. It might be better if you were a registered nurse, but it's not essential. Your contacts, to be honest, are more valuable.' He waited a beat. 'Assuming, of course, that the police weren't involved?'

'No!'

He held a hand up. 'No offence intended.' He pulled a keyboard closer and tapped. 'Right, how about tomorrow at midday?'

Jodie looked at him blankly.

'For an interview with the company? If they're interested, which I'm sure they will be.'

This was all happening too fast. Jodie had always hated rollercoasters, the sensation of the world falling away beneath her feet, the heart-in-your-mouth feeling, the being out of control. A little over a week ago, her life was solid. Now it was vapour.

'Tomorrow at midday.'

'Great,' Bisby said, taking her words as assent. 'Let me get on to them and see if I can get that set up.'

Mesmerised, Jodie listened to him speak about her, hardly recognising the description he was giving to whoever was listening on the other end.

'Great, she'll be there.' Bisby hung up with a grin splitting his round face. 'That's all set. Graham is looking forward to meeting you, he said you sounded like what they needed.'

And that was it. Bisby gave her a slim folder with information about the company. 'Have a read of that. They may ask what you think of the company, what you know about them. It's good to have answers ready, okay?'

She took the folder. 'Thank you.'

'I'll be in touch tomorrow afternoon. They don't hang about making decisions.' Bisby got to his feet and stretched across the desk to take her hand. 'It's the biggest pharmaceutical company in the city so it would be an excellent opportunity for you. Best of luck with it.'

It wasn't until Jodie was on the train back to Gravesend that she opened the folder. There were several pages, some with diagrams of sales figures, market share, potential expansion, some detailing the structure of the company.

The company. The name made Jodie's head spin.

London Medical. The pharmaceutical company where Flynn worked.

22

Jodie swore under her breath. It couldn't be the same company. She fished in her bag for the card Flynn had given her and took it out. A simple matt black card with his name in large letters across the top, his mobile number underneath and stretched across the bottom... London Medical.

She laughed in disbelief, the sound loud enough to draw attention from a woman further down the carriage who looked at her warily before turning away.

The phone number of the recruitment agency was in her mobile. She'd ring Nate Bisby and tell him she'd changed her mind. It had been a crazy idea anyway.

Crazy. But why then did she feel such disappointment? Perhaps because he'd said that being a nurse wasn't essential... after all, if the NMC ruled against her she might not be one for much longer. She flicked the corner of Flynn's card. It would be no harm in going along for the interview. They probably wouldn't offer her the position anyway, but it would be good experience.

By the time the train reached Gravesend, she'd finished reading the information in the file. It seemed such a great company to work for. No wonder Flynn loved it. She debated ringing him to tell him, maybe even get some advice, but decided against when she remembered how negative he'd been about the idea. He might be even less keen on the idea of her working for the same company.

She could ring Rivka or any of her other girlfriends for advice but she knew what they'd say... that she shouldn't make a decision about her future based on pleasing a man she barely knew, and one who may drift out of her life as quickly as he'd drifted in. It was exactly what she'd have said to them in the same situation.

Her thoughts stuck on the job conundrum, she walked on automatic and was barely aware she'd turned into Wilfred Street. Only when she was standing outside her house with the key in her hand did she notice the package hanging from the door. 'Shit!' she said, stepping backwards, stumbling from the kerb onto the road. Like the last package, this one was blue, neatly tied with a matching ribbon, a loop of which hung over the doorknob, the slight breeze billowing down the street making it sway gently.

Jodie looked up and down the street. Was Victor standing somewhere watching? 'Bastard!' She shouted the word, it echoed and drew no answer.

The package taunted her. She yanked it from the doorknob and flung it away as far as she could, then opened the door and hurried inside. But there was no comfort on that side of the door. She pictured the shoes, lying there, perhaps being run over by a passing car or being drenched from the threatening rain. With a cry of frustration, she went back out, ran to pick the package up and took it inside.

Already the ribbon was grubby, and the neat parcel dented from where it had hit the road. She dropped it on the table and looked at it, anger fizzing through her veins. She'd really had enough.

It was several minutes before she reached for it, undoing the ribbon with trembling hands. The contents were no surprise. Two blue baby shoes. These even smaller, more delicate than the last. Jodie took them out, held them in one hand. So tiny.

Why was Victor doing this?

Revenge for her part in his sentence?

She'd had no choice. And she knew from their solicitor that Victor had been given none either, giving up the rights to his child in return for a lighter sentence. Maybe he held her and her mother responsible for that and the shoes were a symbol of loss.

She pushed her hair back with an unsteady hand. Impossible to know what he meant. As a fourteen-year-old child, she'd adored Victor but she didn't know a thing about the man he was now. He obviously knew where she lived... why didn't he simply knock on her door?

Because he wanted to make her suffer. It was the only explanation. Perhaps Emma Carlton was right and she should go to the police. They might have found one pair of baby shoes amusing, perhaps the delivery of the second would have more impact. Or would they simply dismiss it as a foolish prank that wasn't causing any harm.

Jodie held the shoes to her cheek, feeling the softness. A symbol of loss. A reminder of what they'd had. What they'd made together. A baby boy, born, despite what everyone had said, of their love.

She put the shoes on the table, crossed her arms around them, and laid her head down and wept.

23

Jodie allowed herself a few minutes' self-pity before straightening. She was tempted to throw the baby shoes out. It would have been the sensible thing to do but, instead, she brought them upstairs, put them with the others, and shut the lid of the box with a snap. She was tired trying to second-guess Victor. She'd no idea what he hoped to achieve by sending her the damn shoes... if it were simply to unsettle her, he was doing a good job.

She'd like to have spoken to Flynn but wasn't sure she could keep the sadness from her voice so was half glad, half disappointed when he sent a text rather than ringing.

I hope you're missing me. Looking forward to seeing you on Wednesday.

It wasn't quite as satisfying as hearing his voice, but it cheered her a little all the same and she considered ringing him for all of two seconds before deciding against it. She might be tempted to tell him about the interview and, worse, who it was with.

They barely knew each other. He didn't think she was tough enough to be a sales rep, but then, he knew little about her.

She read his text again and tapped out a reply, keeping it simple.

Yes, and me too, x

Determined to do her best at the interview the following day, Jodie picked up the file she'd been given, read through the information again and did an internet search to see what else she could find out. Everything she read was good. They seemed to be a great company to work for, but she'd already known that thanks to Flynn.

Flynn. He was special. She'd never felt this right with someone and she'd been searching for a long time. There was something about him that appealed to her. She'd be honest with him... about everything... eventually.

Dinner was a frozen pizza and a glass of wine on the sofa in front of the TV. She watched a documentary but switched it off when her attention wandered and curled up with her eyes shut instead. Questions popped into her head almost instantly. What was she going to do about Victor? How many shoes was he going to send before giving up?

Her tired and muddled brain couldn't answer. She dragged herself up to bed, slipped naked under the duvet and rolled over to the side where Flynn had slept. His scent gave her comfort, and despite her worries she fell asleep.

It was the beep-beep of a van reversing outside that woke her. She listened to it; to the faint sound of distant traffic and the gentle pattering of rain against the window. Her world sounded normal. But it wasn't. Reluctantly she opened her eyes, surprised to see it was 9am. She hadn't slept so well in days. It was time to get up, get breakfast, read over that information again. Plan some questions to ask at the interview. Get on with her life.

An hour later, wearing a plain white shirt and navy trousers, she sat with a mug of coffee and skimmed through the file, jotting down key points, and framing some questions to ask.

The headquarters of London Medical was in Ealing. She did an internet search, located the address, and planned her journey. Almost an hour and a half. She checked her watch. Time to get ready to leave.

The worst of the rush hour was over but the train station was still busy. Afraid of being dragged into a seam of paranoia where she saw Victor in every face, Jodie kept her head down, and concentrated on the meeting ahead. The journey was uneventful. She crossed from St Pancras International to Kings Cross and caught the Piccadilly line to Holborn, changing there for the Central line to Ealing Broadway. Her destination a ten-minute walk from the station.

She'd allowed thirty minutes extra time for delays which hadn't occurred. Locating the headquarters building, she checked the time again, then looked around for somewhere to wait. A café across the street seemed the perfect solution. She sat with a cappuccino and kept her eyes on the front door of the building, hoping to catch a glimpse of Flynn coming or going. She gathered he didn't spend much time in the office, but she might be lucky.

At five to the hour, she stood, straightened her jacket and backbone, left the café, and dashed through the traffic to the front door of the office building.

Inside, a glossy reception area held several chairs and a desk staffed by one elegant woman of indeterminate age who looked up from her computer as Jodie approached.

'I have an appointment with Graham Barker.'

The woman looked at a clipboard on her desk. 'You must be

Jodie Armstrong. Welcome to London Medical.' She indicated the chairs behind with a wave of beautifully manicured fingernails. 'Please, take a seat and I'll tell him you're here.'

Jodie had barely sat before a door to one side opened and an attractive man with grey-streaked dark hair and a disarming smile crossed to her with his hand extended.

'Ms Armstrong, welcome to London Medical.'

His grip was firm and dry. She felt the tension ease and managed a smile in return. 'Thank you.'

'My office is on the next floor, if you'll follow me.'

He made small talk about the weather and her journey from Gravesend as they waited for the lift. She tried to think of something intelligent and clever to say but couldn't think of anything more interesting than there'd been no delays.

'Good, good,' he said, waving her ahead of him into the lift when it arrived, and out on the first floor. 'Through here.'

The office was large and bright. Jodie sat on the chair indicated, dropped her bag to the floor, then hurriedly picked it up to take out the pen and notepad she'd brought, dropping it again, feeling a little flustered.

Graham Barker was rocking his swivel chair slightly. 'Why don't you tell me about yourself.'

I had a child when I was fourteen and I think I'm being stalked by the man responsible. The thought almost made her smile, and it did make her relax. 'I qualified as a nurse sixteen years ago. I spent several years working in operating theatres in Dubai and got to know several anaesthetists there who I've stayed friendly with. It was their idea that I should pursue a position as a sales representative.' It was a lie, but he'd never know that. She spoke about her time in Dubai, her decision to come back to the UK and her desire for a change in career.

Barker nodded encouragingly throughout.

'And that's about it,' Jodie said finally. She didn't mention getting fired, or the investigation by the NMC. If he offered her the job, they could discuss it then.

'Good, good. And what made you choose London Medical?'

She guessed he didn't want to hear her say it was the first position she was offered. Nate Bisby had told her it was all about contacts. It seemed a good idea to use what she had. 'Once I'd decided on a sales career it seemed a good idea to work for the best. I have a friend who works for London Medical. He absolutely loves what he does so it seemed to be the perfect reference.'

Barker's eyebrows rose. 'A friend?'

'Yes, Flynn Douglas. He's worked here for several years.' She waited for the nod of acknowledgement at the mention of one of their own. But instead, Barker's head tilted in a question.

'Flynn Douglas?'

'Yes.' She reached for her bag, pulled it to her and searched inside for the card she'd looked at so carefully the day before. 'Here,' she said, holding it forward.

Barker took it, eyes narrowing as he looked at it, the corners of his suddenly thin lips turning downward. 'Have you known this... Flynn Douglas... long?'

The ice in his voice sent a band of tension tightening around Jodie's head. She gulped and stared at his now stern, unfriendly face. There was something terribly wrong. It seemed a good time to be honest. 'Two weeks.'

Barker tapped the card. 'We don't have anyone called Flynn Douglas working at London Medical.' He reached into a drawer, took out a business card and slid it across the desk. 'These are what our cards look like. As you can see, the company logo of an intertwined L and M are quite distinctive.'

Jodie picked up the grey card with trembling fingers. It *was* a distinctive design. There was no similar logo on Flynn's card. 'Maybe I've made a mistake, maybe it's a different company.'

She wasn't really surprised when Barker shook his head. 'That's impossible. And I have to admit I'm a little concerned that this man appears to be pretending to work for us.'

A little concerned? Jodie was flabbergasted, stunned. 'I'm sure there is a reasonable explanation,' she said, trying to think by any stretch of the imagination what it could be.

Barker's narrowed eyes pinned her to the chair. 'I'm afraid I'll have to insist on your finding out what that is and informing me. Otherwise I will have no option but to involve the police.' He picked up the matt black card. 'If someone is impersonating a London Medical representative, it could have serious repercussions for us and for our customers' trust in the company.' He got to his feet. 'I'll give you till this time tomorrow to find out what's going on before I decide whether I need to drag us into what might be a very messy situation.'

Jodie blinked, her mouth dropping open in wordless dismay. There was no further discussion about her working for them, no warm handshake as Barker waved her from his office, no chat as they went down in the lift, no pleasant goodbye as he opened the front door, closing it firmly after she'd gone through as if to say she wasn't welcome back.

Shock numbed her brain. Afterwards, she couldn't remember walking back to the train station, switching from the Central to the Piccadilly line or crossing the busy junction to catch her train home.

It was only as she pushed open the door into her house that the shock started to wear off. Anger galloped in on its tail and she stomped into the kitchen, threw her bag against the wall, and screamed every expletive she could remember. Flynn and Victor: both came under the lash of her tongue.

What an idiot she'd been. Hadn't she known there was something too good to be true about Flynn? And there was that story about his apartment... she'd been right, she knew it now, he'd spoken about his spacious apartment until she suggested going there, then suddenly it was too small. Lies. All ugly lies.

She picked up her bag and grabbed the contents that had fallen out including the notebook that she'd never had reason to use. She looked at it sadly before crossing the kitchen and throwing it in the bin.

Early as it was, wine seemed like a good idea. There was an open bottle in the fridge. She took it out and slopped some into a glass, filling it to the brim, slurping some when it lapped over the edge as she crossed to the table and sat heavily. Another gulp was needed when she felt tears sting. She was damned if she was going to cry over the bastard.

The best thing to do was to simply cut Flynn off. Tomorrow, when Graham Barker didn't hear from her, he'd contact the police. Let him! It would serve Flynn right for his deception. For making her believe.

Her glass was almost empty before she'd calmed and remembered that Flynn was calling there that night. Part of her wanted to confront him, to see his expression when she told him she knew about his lies and to ask him why. But it didn't really matter. He *had* lied, and she could never trust him again.

It would probably be better to send him a text, say she'd changed her mind and didn't want to see him again. *Never wanted to see him again.* Despite his lies, the thought saddened her.

In the end, she did nothing apart from switching off her phone. The recruitment agent said he'd ring. She didn't want to have to explain the fiasco of an interview.

The wine glass was empty, she refilled it and this time brought the bottle to the table and sat drinking until the light began to fade. She'd no idea of the time and when the doorbell rang, her hand jerked, sloshing wine over her fingers. It trickled down her arm as she held the glass and listened to the bell sounding again. Then Flynn's voice as he pushed open the letterbox flap and called through. He sounded vaguely puzzled rather than worried. She imagined him there, his handsome face creased as he tried to figure out what could be wrong. Maybe the wrong day, or the wrong time.

She put her glass down and crossed to the open kitchen door, straining to hear. The murmur of his voice reached her. He was probably ringing her, leaving her a message, maybe laughing at the confusion of being there when it appeared she wasn't.

Slow, quiet steps took her to the front door, clamping down on the yell that almost escaped when he rang the doorbell again. With a lump in her throat and a pain in her chest, she rested a shoulder against the wall. He didn't give up easily, ringing the doorbell now and then, and occasionally she heard the murmur of his voice as he left yet another message for her. Perhaps it was her imagination, but a hint of panic seemed to be creeping into his words.

It was almost an hour before she heard his footsteps move away. She rested against the door then, her wet cheek sliding against the cold uPVC, bitter sadness in every heaving breath. Anger would come, and hate too, but not until the pain of his lies had faded.

Back in the kitchen, she sat looking out the window as the solar lights came on. Pockets of light in the darkness. That's what Flynn had been for the last two weeks, a little light in her increasingly dark life. Now he was gone.

Alcohol was making her maudlin. For goodness' sake, she'd only known the guy a couple of weeks and, as it turned out, it appeared she didn't know him at all. In a few days, he'd have faded like a bad dream.

The idea of taking a position as a sales rep was daft anyway.

She was a nurse. She'd apply for that part-time job, be cleared by the NMC, and get on with her life.

Her phone was sitting on the counter. Her eyes flicked to it. What had Flynn said when he'd rung? Maybe he'd guessed that she knew about his lies and his messages would be littered with excuses. It was tempting to reach for it and switch it on to listen. But she'd had enough for one day.

Leaving it where it was, she took herself upstairs and, still in her interview-appropriate clothes, she lay down on her bed and shut her eyes.

24

Victor was puzzled. He'd followed Jodie to the office in Ealing. Her expression was bright, excited even on her way in, but less than twenty minutes later a different woman came out. One with the weight of the world pressing her into the pavement. Every step appeared to be a struggle.

Victor guessed the visit was linked to her attendance at the recruitment office the day before. Perhaps she was considering a change of job. But if her expression was anything to go on, her visit hadn't been a success.

Back in Gravesend, she went inside her home and didn't come out. There had been no sign of lover boy since Monday morning, it might be that he was due that night. Victor would go home and return to his usual spot around 6.15pm and keep watch.

He wasn't sure of his next step. If he were being honest with himself, which wasn't one of his strengths, he'd admit that finding Jodie – following her and learning everything about her – had initially been pure curiosity. But it had grown into an obsession.

They'd labelled him a rapist but it wasn't true. Back then, when he was a gawky twenty-eight-year-old, he found his peers difficult to communicate with. But young girls listened to him, admired him, made him feel good about himself so it was no wonder he'd gravitated towards them.

When Jodie told him she was pregnant, he had been appalled, and horrified too that the adoring expression she normally gave him held a hint of fear. So, he'd spun a vision of their future with the baby, made pie-in-the-sky plans that she lapped up and wallowed in. And her adoration had resumed. Unemployed and living at home, having to part with most of his benefits for his keep, he'd little spare cash to buy Jodie gifts but he'd taken some money from his mother's purse and bought Jodie the baby shoes. The white-and-pink shoes, oddly, were more expensive so he'd settled for blue.

He still remembered her look of excitement when she'd opened the clumsily wrapped gift. She'd laughed and taken them out, cooing over their size. 'It's bound to be a boy,' she'd said, holding them over the barely visible swelling of her belly.

Jodie wouldn't have forgotten them and when he wanted to leave something to show her that he was keeping an eye on her, the baby shoes were the first things that popped into his head. The first pair he'd left was to tell her he was there, the second... that was to show her that he wasn't going to give up.

An obsession – or maybe, he was simply enjoying himself for the first time in his miserable life.

~

At 6.15pm, he was back in position on the corner of Wilfred Street for what might be a long wait.

But he was in luck. Only fifteen minutes later, he saw lover boy turn into the street looking cheerful. There was a bounce in his step, a holdall dragging one arm down and bobbing against his calf as he walked. At Jodie's door, he pressed the doorbell and waited.

Hoping for a shag, Victor thought, his top lip turning up in a sneer. Sex held little allure for him. It was too messy. He waited for

Jodie's door to open, curious to see if she had recovered from whatever had got her down earlier.

To his surprise, the door stayed shut despite lover boy ringing again. When there was still no answer, Victor watched him bend down and lift the letterbox flap. He shouted something through and straightened with what looked like confident expectation.

But the door remained shut.

Trouble appeared to have invaded paradise. Victor didn't believe in coincidence. This had to have something to do with Jodie's meeting earlier. He watched as the man took out his phone, probably to ring her. He didn't know what Victor was sure of, that she was inside, and there was something satisfying in having knowledge that this arrogant younger man didn't have.

Victor gave into sudden temptation and walked briskly down the street. On the same side. He'd be close enough to Jodie's lover to breathe the same air.

'You locked out?' he said when he reached her house, his voice dripping with sympathy that he hoped didn't sound as fake to the younger man as it did to him.

'No, a simple mix-up with my girlfriend.'

'I hope it gets sorted soon.' Victor looked up at the twilight navy-blue sky. 'Forecast is for rain tonight.' He'd no idea what the forecast was but it sounded knowledgeable. He walked on.

At the other end of the short street, he continued around the corner, turned and peered back. He'd be safe there until the man decided to give up and go home.

Victor watched him for a moment then pulled back and leaned against the wall of the house. What could have gone wrong between them? He'd seen Jodie with other men, but he'd been afraid this one might have been more serious. No other man had stayed over more than one night, no other man had arrived with a packed bag as if they planned to stay for even longer. It looked as though it might have ended, but Victor's interest was piqued... what was it about this man *that had fascinated Jodie until today. And even more interesting, what had he done to upset her?*

Victor waited until the man headed his direction before hurrying away and taking cover in a doorway further along the street.

But when lover boy was at a safe distance, Victor followed. It was time he found out more.

25

Jodie didn't sleep but she didn't expect to. Instead, she lay wide awake as thoughts and worries swirled through her head. If she went downstairs, she knew she'd listen to the messages Flynn had left and she couldn't face that yet. In the morning... in the cold light of reality that came with the dawn... then she'd be able to.

She had forgotten to shut the curtains but it wasn't sunshine that made her open her eyes, the morning being grey and dull and her room still in semi-darkness. It was the grim, gloomy inevitability of her life. She'd get over Flynn... because she had to... she'd find some way of dealing with Victor... again because she had to ... and she'd apply for, and take when offered, that part-time nursing position.

But lying there, feeling sorry for herself wasn't going to achieve anything. She sat up and swung her feet to the floor, frowning at the dirty mark her shoes had left on the duvet cover, annoyed with herself for being so sloppy... for being so very, very stupid.

She stood abruptly and turned to pull the cover and sheets off the bed. Keeping busy, that was the key.

~

Thirty minutes later, dressed in jeans and a T-shirt, she had packed the washing machine. Its churning and humming, followed minutes later by the rumble of the kettle boiling, were relaxing sounds of normality.

Normal too was Jodie's breakfast of toast and coffee, the toast because she thought she should eat, the coffee to keep her awake. When she'd finished one of the slices, she pushed the other away and stood to get her laptop from the sitting room.

She sipped her coffee while she tapped out a reply to the nursing home saying she'd be interested in the part-time position and added that she was available for an interview whenever they wished, and happy to start as soon as they wanted. If they invited her for an interview, she'd explain her circumstances. Her union rep had said there was no reason she couldn't accept another post pending the decision of the NMC. She hoped the nursing home felt the same way.

Now, she had to wait for their reply.

Her mobile was on the counter behind her. There was nothing else she could do. It was time to find out what Flynn had said.

She picked the phone up and stared at it for several moments, clamping her lips together when they started to tremble, determined she wasn't going to shed any more tears. Her thumb slid along to the button and pressed. There were eight missed calls, seven voicemails and several texts. Leaving Flynn's for last, she listened to a voicemail from the recruitment agent, Nate. He sounded puzzled and asked her to give him a ring to discuss the interview. She guessed Graham Barker hadn't yet told him the situation. She deleted the voicemail, and his contact details. He'd get the message.

A missed call from Rivka would be her friend ringing for a

chat. Jodie would call her later and fill her in on the latest chapter in her increasingly ridiculous life.

Then it was down to the ones from Flynn. The first voicemail was shortly after he arrived at her door. Three more followed in quick succession, increasingly worried and puzzled. The next, if the voices and background sounds were any indication, was made on the train on his way home. And the final voicemail she guessed was in his apartment, the background quiet, his voice sombre. *'I don't know what's happening, Jodie. Please ring me. I'm worried about you.'*

His text messages echoed the voicemails until a final one sent early that morning.

I thought we had something special. Maybe I was fooling myself. I don't understand how you could simply cut me off like this. Please get in contact, tell me what I did wrong.

Aha! She put the phone down on the table and pushed it away. *What I did wrong.* She grabbed the phone and without thinking, sent a text.

You lied to me.

Then she deleted his details and blocked his number. She wished it were as easy to delete him from her head.

The day loomed ahead of her. It was tempting to ring Rivka and see if she would be free for lunch but she was afraid to... afraid she'd break down and sob at the mess her life had become.

A ping told her she had an email and she was surprised when she looked to see it was a response from the nursing home asking when she'd be free to go for an interview. Why not today? She sent off an email saying she'd be happy to attend whenever suited but that she was free the rest of the day. The reply came several minutes later.

An interview at 2pm. Something going her way.

The jacket and trousers she'd worn the previous day were too creased to wear. She did a quick search through her wardrobe, discounting most of her clothes as being too casual, finally settling on a fine-knit white jumper and beige skirt. Her tan raincoat on top and she'd look okay.

There were hours to get through first. She made her bed, unpacked the washing machine, drank copious amounts of coffee, and read a crime novel by one of her favourite writers. But even Jenny O'Brien's latest couldn't stop her thoughts from drifting to Flynn, to the *what might have been* and to the aching sense of loss.

The nursing home was about a twenty-five-minute walk away. Determined to make a good impression by arriving enthusiastically early, she pulled her raincoat on at 1.15pm, grabbed her bag and keys and opened the front door.

She'd been so lost in thoughts of Flynn, so full of gut-churning self-pity that for a while she'd put the other man who was haunting her out of her mind and was caught by surprise to find a package swinging from the doorknob. More damn shoes! Anger flared. She pulled the package from the door, flung it on the hallway floor and stepped outside.

Tension gripped Jodie, quick jerky steps taking her down the street. This time, she promised herself, this time she'd take the damn package to the police, get them to find Victor and make him stop.

In exactly twenty-five minutes, Jodie reached the nursing home. *Seacrest Manor*. They'd used artistic licence with the name, the sea was at least a fifteen-minute walk away but none of the nursing homes in Gravesend were foolish enough to use the town's name in their title. She tried to put both Flynn and

Victor out of her mind. It was important to make a good impression, to show the manager that she was exactly the kind of nurse he needed... despite having been fired.

To her surprise and relief, the interview went well. Her explanation regarding the medication issue and NMC investigation was accepted without more than a shake of the manager's head and a few easily answered questions.

'We'd like to offer you the position,' the manager said at the end of a short interview. 'Subject to references, of course.'

Jodie's face fell. Stupidly, with all that was going on, she'd not thought about references. 'I've worked for BestLife Care for six years.'

'That's fine.' The manager's voice was calm and reassuring. 'A reference from them to say you've been a satisfactory employee until recent events will suffice, and perhaps one from your time in Guy's?'

'Yes.' Jodie nodded, relieved. 'That would be easy.'

'The permanent post will depend on the results of the NMC, you understand?'

She lifted her chin and kept her eyes unwaveringly on him. 'I assure you, there was no culpability on my part.'

'Right,' he said, dropping his gaze to the paperwork on the desk. 'We can do the DBS check online now. And if you can give me, or send me, the contact details for the referees, I'll get that done as soon as.' The manager wasn't a man who let grass grow anywhere. He looked up and caught her amused expression. 'You'll learn, I'm not someone who likes to hang about.'

The Disclosure and Barring Service check took five minutes to complete. When they'd finished, Jodie gave the manager the email address of an anaesthetist she worked with in Guy's who she knew would happily give her a glowing reference. 'And Kate Dobson at BestLife Care.'

'I know Kate,' he said. 'Don't worry. You've told me about the

NMC investigation. All I want to know from her is that you're reliable, efficient and competent.'

'Which I am,' she said firmly.

'Excellent. If the references come through perhaps you could start next week.' He picked up what Jodie saw was a duty roster. 'We need someone for Saturday and Sunday.'

'Perfect,' she said. And less than forty-five minutes after arriving, she walked from Seacrest Manor feeling that one part of her life was sorted.

She planned to go directly home to ring the police about the package but she was suddenly weary, her eyes felt gritty and the thought of having a protracted conversation about Victor seemed simply too much. The package could stay unopened where she'd thrown it until the following morning.

The day had brightened. Jodie walked along Saxon Shore Way but she'd not gone far when she realised she was simply too exhausted and turned for home. A faint unpleasant smell when she opened her front door made her screw up her nose. She peeled off her raincoat, hung it and her bag over the banister and lifted her nose to sniff the air. It was an odd smell. She took a step forward, stopping as the odour intensified and looked down in horror at the package near her feet.

She hadn't noticed when she'd pulled it from the door earlier, or maybe it hadn't happened until it had hit the floor and broken whatever was inside. Something that stained the corner of the wrapping paper. Jodie bent down and sniffed, straightening quickly. It was a stench she recognised from wounds that were deteriorating... putrid and nasty.

Later, she thought she should have rung the police and left them to deal with whatever it was. But that was when the shock had worn off. Now, with her eyes wide, she bent and picked the package up by one of its ribbons and carried it to the draining board in the kitchen. She took scissors from the drawer and cut the paper, then the tape that held the box shut. It looked the same inside as the last two: the same blue tissue paper.

It had rained earlier, maybe the package had simply got caught in rainwater dropping from the gutters overhead. And the smell was... no, she couldn't think of any reason for the stink that emanated from the open box. Using the points of the scissor blades she parted the tissue paper gently.

The scissors went flying across the room as she leapt away with a horrified yelp and stood trembling, her eyes never leaving the box. 'Fuck!' She held a hand to her mouth, feeling weak, stunned.

It was seconds before she could move, before she could stagger into the hallway, sit on the stairs and fumble inside her bag for her mobile. Then she pressed nine, three times.

'Police,' she said when asked what service she required. In a voice almost devoid of intonation, she told the police operator her story, answered the questions she was asked and slumped on the stairs when she was told an officer would be around within the hour.

Jodie didn't move while she waited. A wave of self-pity rolled over her, and she gulped, pressing her lips together to prevent a howl of anguish. She picked up her phone and sent Rivka a text.

If you're not doing anything tomorrow, could you come around. I need to talk to you.

Her friend had Fridays off; she hoped she'd not made other plans.

A few minutes later, her phone buzzed.

Sure, eleven okay?

Perfect, See you then.

Relieved, Jodie put the phone down.

When the doorbell rang, slightly less than an hour since her emergency call, she stood shakily and went to let them in. She had her hand on the doorknob, then stopped and pressed closer to the door to listen for voices. It was quiet. 'Hello?'

'Ms Armstrong, it's the police.'

Of course it was. Shaking her head, she twisted the handle and pulled open the door. Two uniformed officers stood outside, their car parked across the road. 'Sorry,' Jodie said, 'I seem to be getting a little paranoid.'

'No harm in being careful,' the taller of the two men said. 'My name is PC Robert Doyle and this—' he indicated the other officer '—is PC Joe Grant.' When Jodie made no move to wave them in, he smiled slightly. 'May we come in?'

Colour flared across Jodie's cheeks. 'Yes, of course.' She stood back and indicated the sitting-room door. 'We can sit through there. Would you like a drink?'

'No, thank you.' Doyle appeared to be the officer in charge, it was certainly he who did all the talking.

The two men were big, muscular rather than fat, tall and broad, and they filled the small room. They perched on the edge of the sofa as Jodie sat on the small chair in the corner opposite.

Doyle took out his notebook, flicked it open, then shut it again. 'You received a nasty package in the post?'

Jodie frowned and shook her head. 'No, not in the post. It was left hanging on the doorknob. There have been others, two others, but they had little shoes inside... baby shoes... this one was...' She held her hand over her mouth and gulped frantically.

The two officers, with the air of men who'd seen it all before, waited patiently, as she tried to get herself under control. 'Take your time,' Doyle said.

Jodie shook her head. Words were too difficult. 'I'll show you.'

She led the way to the kitchen, her hand hesitating on the door handle. What if there was nothing there? With so much stress recently, had she imagined it all? 'It's been a strange few weeks,' she said, turning to look at the men who stood too close behind her. Suddenly claustrophobic, she pushed the door open and stepped inside. 'There.' It was almost a relief to see it still on the draining board, to know it was real.

It looked so innocent. Such a pretty shade of blue. From the doorway, the staining wasn't visible. Nor was the content.

When she didn't move, Doyle squeezed past and crossed the room. He peered inside. 'All I can see is paper,' he said, pulling a disposable glove from his pocket. He slipped it on and slowly moved the wrapping back. 'Ah.'

Only one word, but it was enough to make Grant put a hand on Jodie's arm to move her to one side.

His reaction to the contents was more dramatic than his partner's. He reared back. 'Bloody hell.'

Doyle turned to Jodie. 'Do you have the other items that were sent?'

'Yes, I'll get them.'

A few minutes later, the two officers were examining the baby shoes.

'And these are the ones given to me by Victor Hill.' Jodie pushed the box forward.

Doyle opened the box and took them out, the shoes tiny in his big hands. 'And they were never used?' He looked at Jodie curiously.

'No, my baby was put up for adoption. I never saw him.' Jodie felt a lump in her throat. Those words never got easier to say.

Doyle put the shoes back in the box and tucked the tissue

paper neatly around them. 'Okay, so you believe Hill has started this stalking because he finally managed to get his name removed from the register of sex offenders.'

Jodie wanted to scream that it was blindingly obvious that was the way it went, but she guessed there was no point in taking her stress and misery out on the officer who was simply doing his job. 'Yes, it seems to make sense. Nobody else knew about the shoes.'

'Nobody? Are you sure?' Doyle folded his arms. 'People often think they've kept a secret but when they think about it, they've told one or two people... people who may have then gone on to tell one or two more.'

That night she'd had too much to drink and told Rivka and her other nursing friends... had she mentioned the shoes then or told Rivka about them later? She honestly couldn't remember.

'I can see from your expression that I'm right,' Doyle said with a smugness that made her want to hit him.

'I may have told a couple of girlfriends, years ago, but they'd never do something like this. Why would they?'

'People don't always need a reason to cause trouble. Could be any manner of things... jealousy, spite, you name it.' Doyle sat on one of the kitchen chairs. 'Have you told anybody more recently?'

'It's not the kind of thing you simply drop into conversation,' she said, taking the chair opposite.

'And you can't think of anyone who'd want to wish you ill?'

Flynn. Maybe he would now after being dumped so unceremoniously. But he didn't know about her past. 'Oh no,' she blurted out as a thought struck her. 'There is someone, I suppose he might have snooped and found the shoes.' The first night Flynn had stayed over. She'd gone downstairs early, perhaps he'd made the most of her absence and had a look around – learned her secrets. The box where she kept the baby shoes Victor had given her, she distinctly remembered being surprised later that same morning to find it so easily accessible.

'I dumped him because I discovered he'd been lying to me,' she explained.

Doyle frowned. 'Okay, how long have you known this guy?'

'Two weeks, on Tuesday.'

'And the first shoes arrived when?'

'Last Friday.'

'A little over a week after you met this man?'

Jodie gulped and nodded.

'And when was it you dumped him?'

'Last night.' Jodie could see where he was going. Flynn had said he liked her being *needy*. Perhaps he had made her life a nightmare to cast himself as the white knight who would run to her rescue and protect her. 'I was so angry and upset that he'd lied to me, I let him come here as planned, then didn't answer the door or his calls.'

Doyle looked over to where the package still sat. 'Looks like he got his revenge then, doesn't it?'

The image of the mouse with its head chopped off, so neatly wrapped in the blue tissue paper, was seared into Jodie's mind. 'Yes,' she said, 'it looks as if he did.'

26

'Tell me everything you know about this man Flynn,' PC Doyle said, taking out his notebook.

Jodie shook the image of the decapitated mouse from her head with difficulty. 'I only knew him for such a short time, and by the looks of things I didn't really know him at all.'

'Start with his full name, where you met him etc.'

It didn't take long... there was little to tell.

'Kingsman Street, Woolwich,' Doyle repeated, looking at his notebook. 'That's it? No apartment name or number.' He frowned as she shook her head. 'There are hundreds of apartment blocks along that street.' He tapped the notebook against his hand. 'He told you he was a sales rep for London Medical—'

'I had no reason to doubt him, did I?'

'No, but was he lying simply to con you or was this something he'd been doing for a while and if so, to what end?'

'He had business cards, they were hardly done simply to fool me.'

'Possibly not. Do you still have it?'

'No, that sales manager – Graham Barker – he kept it. I have *his* card though.' She stood and went into the hall to pick up her bag, scrabbling inside it as she returned to the table. 'Here you go.' She handed the card over and sat. 'And I have Flynn's phone number, of course.'

'Okay.' Doyle looked up, his pen resting on the page of his notebook. 'What is it?'

Jodie had deleted the details from her phone but the number had stuck in her head like an irritating splinter and she reeled it out without hesitation. 'What happens now?'

'We'll have a word with Mr Douglas, see what his game is. If he did leave the packages, he might admit what he did but he might not.' He looked towards the draining board. 'We'll take that one with us and have it checked for fingerprints.' Doyle looked to his colleague. 'I think that's about it for the moment, unless you can think of anything, PC Grant.'

'No, except we'll need to take Ms Armstrong's fingerprints for elimination purposes.' Grant stood and tilted his head at the door. 'I'll go and get the mobile scanner.'

When he'd gone, Doyle looked at Jodie more kindly. 'I know it's difficult but try not to worry. I'd say your friend Flynn was making a point. Hopefully, you'll never hear from him again.' He hesitated, then as if deciding to be honest, he added, 'I wouldn't be convinced, though, that he was responsible for your problems with your last employer. That seems a bit of a stretch if you don't mind me saying.'

'But you will ask him, won't you?'

'It will be one of the things we'll be asking him,' the officer agreed. 'If Douglas did leave the packages, it's possible that he'll simply be cautioned. Leaving packages on a doorknob, even one with a dead mouse, wouldn't be viewed as a criminal act. We might be able to charge him with a crime if his impersonation of a sales representative was used for financial gain or if it had any other implications.'

'I'm hearing a lot of *ifs*,' Jodie said with a hint of a smile.

Doyle shrugged. 'Until we know more, take the usual precautions, Ms Armstrong, keep your eyes and ears open and stay away from isolated places, especially at night.'

A dart of anger shot through Jodie. Yes, of course, *she* had to be careful because some maniac was sending her dead mice. The anger faded quickly. It was the way life was. 'Yes, I'll be careful. I always am.'

The sound of footsteps heralded the return of PC Grant with the mobile fingerprint scanner and within minutes Jodie's fingerprints had been taken.

'Okay,' Doyle said. 'That's about it. I'll contact you later if we've managed to get hold of Mr Douglas.'

And there was that *if* again. 'Thank you.'

'We'll see ourselves out.'

Jodie listened as their heavy footsteps echoed on the wooden floor of the hallway and the rattle as they slammed the front door. Then there was nothing but the loud thoughts that hammered her skull.

A headache started, throbbing behind her eyes. She pushed to her feet, scrabbled in a drawer for the box of paracetamol she knew was somewhere, becoming increasingly frustrated with her inability to find them... with her inability to make any sense of her messed-up life. Finally, she found the box, popped two and swallowed them with a mouthful of water.

Outside, her small back garden was bathed in sunshine. It was tempting to go for a long walk, to let the sea breeze blow away the stress and get her thoughts in order. But she didn't want to be among people. Despite the realisation that it was Flynn, not Victor who'd been responsible for the packages, she knew she'd be searching every man's face looking for her childhood lover and seeing threats where surely none existed.

Jodie sat and ran a hand wearily over her face. It was almost amusing... if she hadn't been fired, she wouldn't have been looking for a job, and wouldn't have found out what a lying, cheating piece of scum Flynn was. Jodie's mouth twisted at the irony of it all. She wasn't a violent woman, but she wished he were there now so she could show him how strong she was, that someone like him wasn't going to get her down.

The medication trouble in the nursing home was probably someone trying to cause trouble – for the home or for her in particular – she might never find out but as her union rep said, it didn't matter, all that mattered was to get through the investigation without being struck off.

Jodie groaned and rested her head in her hands. It would have been nice if Flynn had turned out to be the man she'd thought he was. Strong as she knew she was, she could have done with a shoulder to cry on, an arm to lean on.

Just for a while.

27

Victor lay on the bed in his pokey bedsit, hands clasped behind his head, his eyes shut. He wasn't asleep but he did his best thinking in the dark.

He'd followed lover boy from Jodie's house, keeping a careful distance. But he needn't have bothered. The man kept his head down the entire journey, only looking up when the train approached. Victor didn't know the details but he guessed, for whatever reason, Jodie had dumped him. Satisfaction shot through Victor at the thought. He'd been right, the man hadn't been at all suitable.

Curiosity lingered, driving Victor to follow him, changing trains, trailing after him until eventually the man left Woolwich Arsenal station and trudged down the street with Victor, a few steps behind, walking slower than he'd thought possible.

He dropped behind when the man turned into the quieter Kingsman Street, then raced to catch up as he headed towards the door of an apartment block. Instinct made Victor reach into his coat pocket for his set of keys and hurry after him, rattling his keys in front of his face, and shouting a cheery, 'Thanks, you can leave it open for me' as lover boy opened the door.

The man didn't turn to look and Victor put his hand on the door before it clicked shut. Lover boy could have let an axe murderer into the apartment block. Victor would have tutted had he not been grinning at the success of his ruse. He listened to the heavy slap-slap of the man's soles echoing on the concrete steps of the narrow stairwell and waited till he'd rounded the first turn before following, slowly and quietly.

On the fourth floor, when the sound of the footsteps faded, Victor ran to catch up. He pushed open the heavy fire door and peered around the edge, swearing softly to see the corridor in each direction empty. He waited a second, then, convinced he heard the rattle of keys, he let the door swing shut and walked towards the sound, reaching the corner in time to look around the edge and see the man disappear inside one of the apartments.

Victor strolled casually down the corridor, noted the number on the door, then retraced his steps downstairs.

In the small entrance lobby, postboxes were set into the wall on one side. All neatly numbered. He located the box allocated to apartment 426 and with a glance around to ensure nobody was entering, slid his fingers inside and fished out the post. Letters to two different people, both men. Mark Tallon and Flynn Douglas.

One of them was the man he followed. Victor memorised the names, shoved the post back into the letterbox and left, humming under his breath.

Back in his bedsit, he pulled out his laptop. Persistence was his biggest strength. He started with Facebook, quickly dismissing the thirty Mark Tallons and the twenty Flynn Douglases. There were, of course, some who didn't include photos but Victor, remembering the smug arrogance of the man, knew he was the type who'd want to show off his handsome face. Victor persevered and an hour later he'd found him.

Victor zoomed in on the photograph. Younger, but there was no doubt. Flynn Douglas. He'd obviously tried his hand at modelling – unsuccessfully – the last photo was dated three years before. A failed model. Victor smirked and sat back. A failure: no wonder Jodie had dumped him.

Victor's curiosity was satisfied. He shut the laptop and lay back to think.

28

On Friday morning, after a night haunted by headless mice chasing her around Cliffe Fort, a red-eyed Jodie didn't bother to get dressed. She pulled on a robe instead and went downstairs to wait for Rivka to arrive. Her friend, as was her custom, was a little late, and as was also her way, rang the doorbell several times, the sound ricocheting in Jodie's skull as she hurried to open the door before the bell was rung again.

Rivka bustled through the open door with a wide smile. 'Sorry I'm late, the phone rang as I was heading out. My mother!'

'Come on, I'll make you some coffee,' Jodie said heading back to the kitchen.

Rivka flopped onto a chair and leaned her elbows on the table. 'She's almost impossible to get away from, I kept telling her I had an appointment.'

'She loves you.'

'Yes, I know.'

There was silence for a few seconds. Jodie kept her attention on what she was doing but she could feel her friend's eyes assessing her.

'You probably know already,' Rivka said quietly. 'But you look like shit.'

Jodie managed a smile at the blunt assessment. She brought everything to the table and sat opposite her friend. 'You'll need caffeine to hear this.' She laughed. 'Actually, you'll probably be wishing for a drink, but I guess it's too early even for us.'

'That bad?'

'Let's say that my life appears to be going from bad to worse.' Jodie lifted her mug and took a mouthful.

Rivka reached across the table and squeezed her other hand. 'Now you're really worrying me. Tell me.'

Jodie took a deep breath and told her friend about her visit to London Medical, her realisation that Flynn had lied to her, the package that had been left the previous morning and the visit by the police. 'Flynn left the first packages so he could be my white knight. And the last as punishment for my dumping him.' She picked up her coffee again and sipped as she watched shock and disbelief flicker across her friend's face. 'Quite a tale, eh?'

'I'm stunned.'

'You can imagine how I felt opening the box, half expecting to find more shoes and finding a mouse instead with its decapitated head resting in a puddle of blood.'

'Stop,' Rivka said, holding a hand over her mouth. 'So, Victor... he wasn't involved with the packages at all.' She frowned as she thought of something else. 'The medication issue in the nursing home... was that Flynn too?'

Jodie played with the handle of her mug. 'I don't think so. Possibly it was someone in the home trying to cause problems and I happened to get caught in the crossfire. Or something.' She held up a hand. 'Nothing seems to make sense so that does as well as anything else.'

'Okay. What now?'

'The police will talk to Flynn. Hopefully, he'll admit it and will be cautioned and told to leave me alone.'

'But he was impersonating someone!'

Jodie smiled at her friend's outrage. 'It depends, seemingly, on why he was doing the impersonation. If it was simply to impress me, then no crime was committed.'

Rivka's eyes widened. 'He left you a decapitated mouse!'

'Revenge for chopping him out of my life, maybe he thought it was appropriate. Anyway–' Jodie reached for the coffee pot and topped up both mugs '–he's out of my life.' She lifted her mug and took a sip. 'Right, let's talk about something else. How's Tasha?'

It was always the perfect question, Rivka switching from the worried friend to the adoring girlfriend in a heartbeat. Jodie answered on cue, asked appropriate questions, and pasted a faint smile in place.

'You're not fooling me, you know,' Rivka said a while later. 'I don't think you've heard a word I said.'

'You were saying how wonderful Tasha is.' It was a safe bet that her friend was saying something along those lines. Jodie smiled when Rivka laughed and nodded. It was impossible to spend time with her and not be cheered up. For goodness' sake, she barely knew Flynn, she shouldn't allow his shenanigans to impact on her so much.

When Rivka was ready to leave, Jodie jumped to her feet. 'Give me two minutes to get dressed and I'll walk to the station with you. I could do with some fresh air and exercise.'

They chatted about nothing in particular as they walked, the way old friends did. At the station, they hugged. 'Thank you for coming,' Jodie said. 'Talking really helped. Flynn will soon be a distant memory.'

'You deserve better.' Rivka hugged her tightly for a second.

'Remember, anytime you need me, I'll be there for you.' Then with a wave she was gone.

~

Jodie felt in a lighter mood after Rivka's visit. It continued until she turned into Wilfred Street, then it plummeted, rocking her on her feet, fingers of fear tightening around her, making her heart beat faster, her breathing hitch.

Leaning against her door, both hands shoved into the pockets of a beige raincoat, stood a man she'd hoped never to see again. As soon as he saw her, Flynn straightened. He kept both hands in his pockets... perhaps he thought it was less threatening... but it wasn't.

Jodie stopped, her eyes flicking from side to side, wondering if she should try to run for it, or if... her hand fumbled for the catch of her bag... she should ring for the police. A spurt of anger fought its way through the fear and strengthened her resolve. She refused to be a victim, to be the needy woman he'd wanted to make of her.

With her chin high, she strode to the door of her house, stopping a few feet away from a grim-faced Flynn. 'What do you want?'

'I had the police on the phone to me, then spent an hour being interrogated by them.' He took a hand from his pocket and ran it through his hair. 'They accused me of leaving threatening parcels on your door–'

'Not threatening,' she broke in. 'At least not at first. But the last one... that mouse, that was threatening, wasn't it?'

'And you think I sent that? Seriously? How could you think such a thing? What did I ever do that you would lie about that?'

Jodie shook her head. 'It wasn't a lie. I found a parcel tied to my doorknob yesterday. There was a dead mouse inside.'

'I didn't send it!' He turned and walked away, long angry strides that took him almost to the corner where he stopped, keeping his back to her, his shoulders heaving.

It was the perfect opportunity. Jodie pulled out her house keys, opened her front door, dashed inside, and slammed it behind her with a triumphant yelp. But her satisfaction was short-lived. Flynn had looked upset... shocked even. She held an ear to the door wondering if he'd come back and was on the other side, or whether he'd kept going and had gone away for good.

She straightened and took a step away. When she heard the letterbox flap open, she whirled around and stared at it.

'Jodie? Jodie, are you there?'

She held her breath.

'Jodie, I'm not going anywhere until I talk to you... convince you I couldn't do such a thing.'

Two steps took her back to the door. 'Why would I believe anything you said? Flynn Douglas, the important sales rep, eh? Except you aren't, are you? You're a liar.' She could hear the bitterness in her words and shook her head. 'Go away, Flynn.' She *wanted* him to leave, it was too hard being close to him, seeing the man she thought he was and trying to remember the reality. He was a liar. 'Please, leave.' The bitterness had faded, her words now laced with sadness and a hint of despair.

'I can't, Jodie. I'm going to stay until you listen to me. You'll find me here in the morning, cold and wet, frozen to your doorstep. Reporters will come and take photos of the poor fool who simply wanted to explain what an idiot he was to the woman he was sure he was falling in love with.'

Falling in love with? Words... they were empty words, easily said, and meaningless when said with a liar's tongue. She should walk away, leave him there, step over his frozen body in the morning. Then she heard heavy rain peppering the uPVC door and, almost without thought, she reached for the catch and pulled it open.

He was standing there, wet hair plastered to his forehead, rain... or tears... running down his cheeks. Jodie felt her heart stumble on a beat as he stepped inside and stood dripping raindrops on the wooden floor, the space between them full of unsaid words and mixed emotions.

'I didn't leave those packages.'

Jodie kept her eyes locked on his brown ones. She'd read somewhere that you could tell when someone was lying – they looked to the right, or maybe the left, she couldn't remember which – but his eyes never moved, looking straight into hers, right into the very heart of her, making it beat faster and stronger.

Flynn wiped rain from his face with his hand. 'I lied to you about my job, but not about that, I swear.'

Jodie indicated the wet floor. 'You're making a mess, you'd better come into the kitchen.' She turned and walked away. A loud sigh tugged at her heartstrings and she knew she was weakening fast.

Flynn took his wet shoes and coat into the small utility room off the kitchen, hanging the coat on one of the pegs and looking around for somewhere to put his shoes before leaving them on the back doormat. He stood in the doorway staring at her, looking ridiculously vulnerable in his socked feet.

'Sit down, for goodness' sake.' Jodie was angry with him for his lie, irritated with herself for her weakness and completely exasperated at the situation they were in. 'I should never have let you in.'

'I'm glad you did,' Flynn said, taking the seat opposite. 'You should have told me about the packages... what you were going through. I thought it was that nursing-home mess that had you stressed and sad.'

Jodie shrugged. 'It was both. The packages started arriving shortly after I met you so...'

'You told the police I was sending them?'

Had she? Hadn't it been the police who'd come to that conclusion? She was so weary. 'The first two weren't distressing, just a silly gift.' It wasn't quite a lie, not exactly the truth. 'But the one yesterday was a dead mouse and it upset me so I rang the police.' She held her hands up. 'They asked me about anyone or anything new in my life, and I told them about you and your lie. It was funny but until then, until they pointed out that the packages had started after I met you, I hadn't thought there was any connec–'

'There isn't,' he interrupted her. 'I swear, they had nothing to do with me.'

Jodie gave a half-smile. 'I believe you. But you did lie about your job.' She saw a mix of emotions chase across his face: shame and sorrow mixed with defiance. 'I went for a job interview with London Medical,' she said and watched the defiance fade away.

'Fine. Yes, I lied, okay?' He got to his feet abruptly, took a few steps across the room and turned to look at her. 'I'm a support worker. In Guy's Hospital.'

'A support worker?'

He pressed his lips together. 'An orderly, a porter, whatever you want to call it.'

'I know what a support worker is,' she snapped. 'But I don't understand why you lied and said you were a sales rep.'

Flynn returned to his seat and sat heavily. 'I'm working on the wards these days but last year I was working in the operating theatres and I used to chat to the sales reps who came in to talk to the anaesthetists. Their jobs sounded so exciting with their conferences and sales meetings in foreign countries. Plus, they always looked smart.' He raised both shoulders, dropping them with a sigh. 'I like talking to people and thought it would be something I could do so I applied for a couple of positions.'

'But you weren't offered a job,' Jodie said when silence stretched too long.

'They didn't quite laugh at me at the interview, but I could tell they wanted to. I didn't have any qualifications and all the reps had degrees and what have you. That's something else I lied about, since I'm being honest, I never went to university. I left school at sixteen, you see.' He straightened the lapels of his jacket. 'I'd spent all my money on a posh suit for the interview and afterwards I went to a pub to drown my sorrows and met a woman. We got chatting, I really liked her and when she asked me what I did for a living I told her I was a sales rep for London Medical.'

'And she was impressed?'

'Yes, especially when I told her I was just back from a sales meeting in Prague and that I was heading to Paris the following week. We went on a few dates but there was no real connection.' Flynn ran a hand over his head. 'The next weekend, I went out and met another woman, and told her the same story.'

'I don't understand why you felt you had to pretend. What's wrong with being a support worker?'

'Nothing, and I like what I do, but it can be a dull, monotonous job and it's poorly paid.' He straightened the knot of his tie. 'When I put on my suit, it's as if I become a different person. I talk to people about sales meetings in Vienna and Copenhagen, and conferences in Boston and New York, and I see them thinking, *wow, this guy is so fascinating*.'

Jodie gave an uncertain laugh. Hadn't she thought exactly that? Would it have made a difference if he'd told her he was a support worker? She didn't think so. His stories were fascinating but it had been his smile and quick wit that had attracted her. 'I bet you could talk about things that happen in Guy's and people would find it equally fascinating,' she said. 'It wasn't what you were talking about that kept me listening to you, it was the way you told the stories.'

'My time as a sales rep has come to an end anyway. That guy that interviewed you, Graham Barker, he rang me and told me he'd report me to the police if I kept on with it.' Flynn wiped a hand over his mouth. 'I knew then, of course, why you'd dumped me. I wanted to explain but you'd blocked me. Then this morning, the police rang. I had to go into the station.' He grimaced. 'It wasn't pleasant but I think I eventually convinced them I'd nothing to do with the packages you'd been getting.'

'And the medication problem in the nursing home? Did you have anything to do with that?'

Flynn looked genuinely shocked. 'You think I'd have got you fired? Why? Why would I do such a thing?'

Jodie felt colour wash over her cheeks. She'd been wrong, her reasoning skewed. 'You said you liked *needy women*, I thought maybe it was your way of keeping me like that.'

He shook his head slowly, frowning. 'That was after you got fired. You sounded so upset that I came straight over. I can't remember what I said, I was simply trying to be supportive. There's nothing wrong with that, is there?' His frown deepened. 'I'm sure I never referred to you as being a *needy woman,* though, that sounds insulting.'

It did, and now she couldn't remember if he had used the expression or not. That evening he'd called over, she had needed his support and he'd given it. He was right, there was nothing wrong with that. 'I'm sorry,' she said. 'Everything's got on top of me recently, my thinking isn't straight.'

'But you do believe me, don't you?'

'Yes.' She'd been stupid and messed up the best relationship she'd had in a long time. Across the table, she saw Flynn's handsome face, his warm brown eyes fixed on hers. There was a hopeful light in them. Maybe she hadn't completely ruined everything.

'I'm sorry for lying to you.' Flynn stretched a hand across the table. 'Do you think we could start again?'

Jodie hesitated before unfolding her arms. Then, slowly, she reached a hand for his, feeling his fingers immediately tighten around hers, the warmth and strength of them.

'I don't know,' she whispered. 'Maybe.'

'Please, and I promise I'll never lie to you again.'

It was then that Jodie should have told him the truth about her life, but she didn't want to spoil the moment.

Anyway, although she didn't know it, it was already too late.

29

Jodie and Flynn talked until their throats were dry by which time all had been forgiven and they were back to where they'd been the previous Sunday. Wine helped lubricate their voices and they talked some more while nibbling on toast, hummus and olives, the best in the line of food that Jodie could provide.

Flynn told her about his childhood, his hard-working mother who'd encouraged him to apply for the job in Guy's and how much he missed her since her death the previous year.

'She was happy working in the hospital and never considered leaving even though she never earned more than minimum wage.' He smiled sadly. 'Everyone loved her: so many people turned up for her funeral, there was standing room only.'

'What about your dad?'

Flynn shrugged. 'He walked out when I was only a baby. Mum never saw him again.'

'He never saw you growing up.' Jodie was horrified. 'How could he simply walk out?'

'Seems they had a row and she told him to take a running

jump.' Flynn laughed. 'I suppose she didn't expect him to take her literally.'

'Must have been hard for her, bringing you up on her own.'

'Yes, he never paid anything towards my care and when she tried to chase him for it, she couldn't find a sign of him. Social services tried too but wherever he'd gone he was out of their reach.'

They were sitting on the sofa, the lights out, Jodie's head on Flynn's shoulder. When she heard his soft, 'What about you?' she thought it was time for the truth… or at least a version of it. 'My dad died of cancer when I was thirteen, so it was just Mum and me. When I was twenty, she had a heart attack. She never recovered and my world fell apart.' She felt his arm tighten around her and took a deep breath. A version of the truth. It would do. 'I got pregnant but didn't feel able to keep the baby and give him the life he deserved, so I gave him up for adoption.'

She felt Flynn move, then the touch of his lips on her hair.

'That was a very brave decision and can't have been easy.'

Jodie heard the echo of her cries, her begging words, felt again the wrench at never having seen the child she'd borne. 'No, it wasn't easy but it was for the best.' She knew she'd given the impression she'd had the baby when she was older, after her mother died. Not as a child, too young to understand the repercussions, but enough to feel loss. She tensed, waiting for him to ask if she had any regrets.

But instead of asking about the past, Flynn caressed her neck with his fingers and said, 'Are you in touch with your son?'

'No, the family who adopted him moved abroad and there was no contact. Anyway, I wanted a clean break, it seemed fairer.' The lie came easily, as it always did. She was an expert in lying to herself and it appeared she wasn't too bad at lying to others either. But now that Flynn knew most of it she could put it behind her. Someday, if they lasted, she might tell him the rest of her story. And about Victor. Maybe.

'I–' Flynn started, a frown creasing his forehead.

Jodie held her hand up to stop him. 'Sorry, do you mind if we don't talk about it anymore.'

He looked for a moment as if he was going to argue, but then shook his head. 'Another day.'

She got to her feet and held out her hand. 'We'd better get some sleep.' She tilted her head. 'I bet you must work some weekends.'

'One in four only, which isn't bad.' He took her hand and stood. 'This weekend isn't one of them.'

'Good.' The light filtering from the street lights outside the window lit up his face. She couldn't remember having seen anything more beautiful. Hand in hand, they walked slowly up the stairs, bumping against each other, reluctant to loosen their grip on one another.

Minutes later, they were between the sheets, skin to skin, and less than a minute after that they were asleep.

Jodie hadn't pulled the curtains. Sometime later, the fat full moon worked its way through the clear night sky, its light bright enough to disturb her. Her eyelids flickered as her weary body warred with a suddenly alert brain. Something was wrong. She was trapped. Her eyes flew open, her body tensing to run, then she laughed softly and very gently moved Flynn's heavy arm off her stomach.

She turned to look at him. This was meant to be. Hadn't she known it from the beginning, that connection with him from the first meeting? The digital clock on her bedside table said 4.15. It was way too early to be awake, but sleep had deserted her. She thought about the unexpected events of the previous day. How fast it had turned from disaster to delight.

Her hand crept over the wiry hairs on Flynn's chest, then she lay back and tucked her hands behind her head. Perhaps she should have told him the full story about the child she'd borne when she'd still been a child herself. She consoled herself by thinking that she hadn't lied... not really.

The digital clock taunted her. 4.20. The room was too bright. Perhaps she'd get back to sleep if she pulled the curtains. Instead, she lay staring at the man in the moon and suddenly thought of Victor.

It must have had been he who had sent the packages... maybe he who had planted the medication.

He'd never tried to contact her in the years since his release. Perhaps if he had, she'd have spoken to him and their past could have been laid to rest. She had never wanted to see him and, until recently, she'd barely given him a thought. Her childish infatuation hadn't outlived the pain of labour, and afterwards she was too consumed with grief for her loss – both of her baby and of her childhood – to think of him. She'd had to grow up quickly and things had never been the same again.

Jodie wasn't a fool. She knew the reason Victor was contacting her now was something to do with his name being removed from the sex offenders register. He could come and go wherever he pleased and, for some bizarre, warped reason, he seemed to want to be where she was.

She stared out at the dark night sky where the man in the moon laughed down on her.

Was Victor out there enjoying his little jokes at her expense, trying to mix up her head with those shoes and that damn mouse? Maybe when he saw he'd failed – when he realised that she was no longer the vulnerable, biddable child she had been – he'd leave her alone. She knew he had to be following her. Watching her every movement. He had to have been one of those thousand unremarkable faces that had passed her by or hovered in the periphery of her vision any time the last few weeks.

An unsettling thought shot through her mind. The police had thought Flynn was to blame for the packages since they'd started to arrive shortly after he came into her life. It was too glaringly obvious a coincidence for them to ignore. But what if Victor had been watching her for weeks, maybe months, and it was only when Flynn came on the scene that he decided to make his presence felt.

Back when she'd been an adoring fourteen-year-old, Victor had vowed undying love. As had she. 'I'll love you forever,' she'd said, starry-eyed. But forever for a child doesn't last long, there's no concept of the following year, the future as remote and as alien as a distant planet.

Victor may have loved her. She'd read a lot over the years about people with abnormal sexual predilections. He probably had loved her as much as he was capable of love. But that was because she was a child, he'd have no interest in her as an adult. The love he'd professed to be unending – it had ended once she grew up – hadn't it?

Hadn't it?

Maybe Victor had really loved her.

And maybe he still did.

30

The unsettling idea that Victor might still be in love with her stayed with Jodie the rest of that weekend. It crossed her mind that she should tell Flynn the truth, explain that she'd been a child when she'd had her baby, that it hadn't happened after her mother had died as she'd allowed him to assume. He might be taken aback but he'd understand. Then she could tell him about her worry that Victor was behind the packages.

But every time she opened her mouth to explain, other words came tripping out. The next day... she'd tell him then... but when Sunday arrived, it was the next day again. They were good together: lots of laughter, warm, loving glances, the constant need for contact between them, a fleeting touch, a caress, an enveloping hug. All so good, she didn't want to spoil it. There would be time enough for the nitty gritty of life to edge its way in.

Sunday afternoon, Flynn insisted they go back to his flat in Woolwich. 'I know I gave you the impression when we first met that I lived in a big salubrious place.' Colour darkened his cheeks. 'I had to back-pedal when you wanted to stay. I couldn't tell you the truth that I share a small apartment with another guy who works in the hospital.'

'I did wonder why you weren't keen on me staying at yours.'

'You'll see why when we get there.' He pulled her into his arms for a hug. 'Just don't condemn me, okay?'

'I promise.' She knew everything about him now. There was nothing to condemn.

Flynn had told her the truth about the apartment. It was incredibly small. But it wasn't the size of the tiny bedroom he had that made Jodie blink with surprise. It was the amount of clothes. The small wardrobe was oozing suits, shirts, and jackets. The only free wall in the room held free-standing shelves, each one stacked with piles of neatly folded shirts, T-shirts, jumpers and jeans.

She ran a hand over a pale-grey jumper and raised an eyebrow. 'Cashmere.'

'I spent every penny I had on clothes to keep up the image. Pathetic, aren't I?'

Jodie stepped closer to him and put her arms around his neck. 'Not pathetic at all.' She kissed him on the cheek. 'You're so handsome, funny and kind but you don't have a great opinion of yourself so maybe it was simply easier to pretend to be someone else.'

Flynn took her hands from his neck and pushed her slightly away from him. 'Are you suggesting I have an inferiority complex?'

'I'm saying you saw those men in their suits with what you perceived to be more glamorous jobs and envied them a little. The same as I envied you and went for that job interview. Truth is–' she smiled '–being a sales rep is probably hard work and the glamour an illusion. All that waiting for someone to speak to you, touting your wares and hoping someone is going to bite.'

Flynn laughed. 'I like the way you look at things. And you're right, of course, sometimes those poor idiots are hanging around for ages and often they're sent off with a flea in their ear.' He pulled her into a tight hug. 'We've known each other such a short time, yet I feel you know me better than any woman I've ever been with.'

'And there've been hundreds, I assume,' she said, joking to lighten the mood.

'Not quite hundreds.' He brushed a strand of hair from her cheek, his fingers caressing. 'And nobody I felt this comfortable with.' His warm brown eyes stared into hers. 'Now that you know all my guilty secrets, there'll be no more lies between us.'

It was the perfect opportunity to explain, and she would have done... she had the words on the tip of her tongue... but then Flynn kissed her and everything apart from him, his fabulous body, teasing fingers and growing erection, went right out of her head.

Two hours later, Flynn, dressed in casual T-shirt and jeans, had packed some of his clothes into a small holdall. 'I'll be able to go straight to work in the morning. When I was wearing my suit, I had to come back here to change first.' He grinned at her. 'If I'd turned up to the job in a suit, they'd have thought I'd lost it.'

Jodie looked around the room. 'It really is a tiny bedroom.' An idea appeared, fully formed in her head. Karma? Perhaps? But hadn't she known – from the very first meeting – that there was something special between them? There didn't seem any point in putting off the inevitable. It was crazy but it was the right thing to do. 'Why don't you move in with me...

permanently.' She pointed to the shelves. 'I might have enough room for all your clothes.'

Flynn dropped the holdall and stared at her, his mouth slightly open. Then he laughed. 'This is mad,' he said, reaching for her, his hands cupping her face. 'Absolutely ridiculous, but yes, that's a bloody marvellous idea.'

With the holdall swinging from Flynn's free hand, they walked arm in arm to the train station giggling and smiling like excited teenagers. Jodie knew she'd done the right thing. Euphoria carried her along and it wasn't until they were crossing the concourse of the train station, swimming against the tide of travellers who'd recently arrived that she remembered she still hadn't told Flynn the truth about her past. He needed to know – what if the packages from Victor kept coming? She'd have to explain somehow, and the longer she left it the more difficult it would be.

Victor. His face was there again in every man of a certain age. Her eyes narrowed as each approaching face in the crowd came into focus, looming towards her, only to be discounted at the last minute. Then her eyes flicked quickly to the next and the next. Not one of these men looked at her, but that didn't make them any less unsettling. Any of them could have been Victor playing a cleverer game. She turned around abruptly, startling Flynn who looked at her with a worried expression.

'You okay,' he said, squeezing her hand, 'you look like you've seen a ghost.'

She returned the pressure. 'Sorry, I thought I saw someone I knew.' And maybe she did, maybe she'd looked right into his eyes as he approached or when she'd turned around. His eyes could be on her right at that moment, his footsteps echoing hers. He could be staring at her hand clasped in Flynn's and thinking about the next stage in his weird campaign to frighten her.

When she pulled her hand away, he stopped, the corners of his mouth downturned. 'You've changed your mind?'

There was a sadness in his eyes that washed away thoughts of Victor. How could Flynn, so charming and handsome, have such poor self-worth? 'No,' she said, reaching for his hand with both of hers. 'I haven't changed my mind at all.'

Any thought of telling him about Victor was dismissed. For all his size, his broad shoulders, his obvious masculinity, Flynn, she decided, wasn't a knight in shining armour who'd rush to fight her battles. That was okay. It was nice to have someone to lean on at times, but she was quite capable of fighting her own. She saw relief banish the sadness from his eyes and reached a hand up to caress his cheek. 'Let's go home.'

Jodie was more than capable of fighting her own battles... and now, she'd fight his too.

31

I t was only when Jodie turned the corner into Wilfred Street that it dawned on her that there could be a package hanging from her doorknob, waiting for their arrival. Her hand was still clasped in Flynn's. She wanted to run ahead and check, like a child, hide the evidence, pretend it never existed.

When they rounded the corner, she tried to keep one step ahead, shielding the front door from view, relief hitting her when she saw nothing there. Maybe it was over, maybe the mouse had been Victor's swansong. 'Almost home,' she said, reaching into her pocket for her keys. She rattled them. 'I've got a spare set, remind me to give it to you.'

Flynn said nothing until they were in the hall, the front door shut behind them. 'What if it doesn't work out? If you're sick of me by the end of the first week.' The words were blurted out as if he'd been chewing on them for a long time.

'Or if you're sick of me.' She threw her coat onto the banisters. 'The future is often far more complicated than we expect, so how about we take every day as it comes.' She waved a hand up the stairs. 'There are two bedrooms. Worst-case scenario, we become friends rather than lovers and stay flatmates. I've considered taking in a lodger more than once.' She hadn't, never needing the money and liking her own space. Sharing with a lover – the intimacy spreading outward from the bedroom so that each meeting, on the stairway, in the bathroom or kitchen, was a reason to touch and kiss – that was a different matter.

Flynn was having doubts, strangely she had none at all.

Flynn went off to work on Monday morning, leaving Jodie curled up under the duvet. She had five empty days ahead of her before she started her new job. She'd laughed at the happy coincidence that her first weekend working was the same one that Flynn worked.

She lay daydreaming for a long time, her thoughts lingering on Flynn but bouncing now and then to Victor despite attempts to relegate him to the furthest, deepest crevice of her mind. Plus, there was the issue of the NMC investigation.

Once that came into her head, she threw the duvet back and got up. Anyway, she had to make space for Flynn and his huge collection of clothes. That thought made her chuckle but a short while later she was frowning. The house was small and she simply didn't have enough storage space. They'd have to get another wardrobe and squeeze it in somehow. She eyed the free wall in her bedroom – maybe something along there? For the moment, she improvised, taking some clothes she rarely wore, folding them into a suitcase and shoving that under the bed. It made some space but not nearly enough for all that Flynn had.

After 9am, she reached for the phone and rang Rivka's mobile. 'You free for lunch?'

'I'm off today,' her friend said sleepily. 'So that would be a yes. Usual place?'

'Perfect. At 12.30?'

'Great, see you there.' The phone went dead.

Jodie spent the next couple of hours rearranging things to make space for Flynn, humming to herself, feeling happier than she had in a while. Not even the occasional invading thought of Victor made a dent in her good mood.

The ring of the doorbell made her frown. She wasn't expecting anyone. Quietly, she slipped the safety chain in place, opened the door and peered out.

'Ms Armstrong, it's PC Robert Doyle.'

Of course, they had promised to keep her informed about the investigation. She shut the door, removed the chain and pulled it open. 'Hi, come in,' she said. He was alone. Across the road she could see his partner had chosen to remain in the squad car. It wasn't going to be a long visit.

Doyle shut the door behind him. 'Just a courtesy call. We spoke to Flynn Douglas. He insists he is innocent of any wrongdoing pertaining to the packages left on your door. He did admit to impersonating a sales rep but as this appeared to be done with no criminal intent, we're not following that up.' He waited for a comment and when Jodie simply nodded, he continued. 'Have you had any further packages?'

'No, there's been nothing. Perhaps whoever was doing it, has moved on to getting his kicks elsewhere.'

'Perhaps.' Doyle's tone of voice was cautious. 'If you do receive more though, don't open them, contact us immediately and we'll be out. As for Douglas, we gave him quite a scare, I don't think he'll be bothering you again.'

'Thank you, and for coming to let me know. That was kind.' Jodie kept the genial expression in place until after the officer had left and she saw their car pulling away. Then she shut the door and let the laughter bubble over. If the ever-efficient PC Doyle knew that not only was Flynn back on the scene but that she'd asked him to move in with her, she guessed he wouldn't be impressed.

~

'You're looking brighter,' Rivka said later, sipping on the glass of wine she'd declared herself in need of.

'I feel it,' Jodie said, smiling.

'Have the police been in touch to tell you they've arrested that Flynn character?'

Was it only Friday when Jodie had been convinced that Flynn was to blame for everything? For a moment, she was struck by how her convictions had changed so rapidly and it worried her. 'Yes, they called around this morning, they've spoken to him but he swore he had nothing to do with the packages. So, I'm going back to my original theory that Victor is behind it all.'

Rivka raised an eyebrow but said nothing as she sipped her wine.

'I'm trying to figure out why. Maybe he wanted to make trouble for me,' Jodie said, almost to herself. 'After all, he served time for his crime. I did none for mine.'

Rivka choked on her wine and thumped herself on the chest. 'You're trying to kill me! Don't be ridiculous, you committed no crime. How many times do I have to say it... you were a child.'

'Yes, I know.' Searching for a motive for Victor's actions was exhausting and worrying. He couldn't simply have walked in and left the tablets, he had to have planned it. And to what end? And having gone to all that trouble, was he going to give up? Jodie caught Rivka's worried expression and shook her head. 'Anyway, let's forget about him, I've much more exciting news to tell you.' She reached for her glass of sparkling mineral water and took a mouthful. 'I asked Flynn to move in with me.'

Luckily, Rivka had put her wine down. No choking this time, instead a shake of her head, eyes wide in disbelief. 'You did what? Are you crazy? Flynn who lied to you, who you were blaming for all your problems just three days ago. That guy?'

'He called around. We had a long talk, he explained everything.' Jodie's eyes softened. 'He's really so sweet and by the end of the night, we were closer than ever. Sometimes,' she said, 'you know when it's right.' Rivka refused to meet her eyes, her mouth a tight line and Jodie sighed. 'You haven't met him yet, but when you do, you'll understand. We have this...' She searched for a word that didn't sound crazy. 'Chemistry, I suppose you'd call it.'

'Lust,' her friend said, meeting her gaze at last and picking up her glass with a shake of her head.

Jodie frowned. 'No, it's not. Yes, he is a wonderful lover but it's not that. We gel. I've never felt this way about someone.' She waited a beat. 'I think I might be in love with him.'

It was Rivka's turn to frown. She put her glass down and leaned closer. 'I've known you a long time and I've never seen you do something so crazy. You were always the sensible one. Remember when I wanted to go off to a kibbutz with that junior doctor I met?'

Jodie laughed. 'Oh, do I remember! You had this romantic idea of what it would be like until I told you that you had to help out with everything and hand over any money you earned. You went off the idea pretty quickly.'

'I'm returning the favour. You barely know this guy. He's already lied to you.' Rivka picked up her glass and drained it, then raised a hand to the hovering waiter and ordered another. 'I probably should have ordered a bottle,' she said with a smile. 'I'm having a lazy day, and meeting Tasha for dinner tonight.' Her smile faded. 'Seriously, Jodie, it isn't that long since you were convinced Flynn was to blame for sending you those packages and somehow involved in that medication fiasco.'

'I was wrong. We had a long talk. He was horrified that I would think that of him.'

Rivka flung her hand up. 'Horrified that you guessed it was him, more like.'

The waiter appearing with the wine stopped conversation momentarily but both women moved restlessly in their seats and when he'd gone, they both spoke at the same time.

'I'm sorry–'

'You don't–'

'You first,' Jodie said, sitting back with her arms folded.

Rivka picked up her glass and took a mouthful. 'I'm sorry if you feel I'm bursting your bubble, but I have to be straight with you. We've been friends, a long time, I don't want to see you hurt.'

'You don't understand, you haven't met him or seen us together.' Frustration made her voice tremble. 'We are made for each other. I remember you telling me about the concept of *yin* and *yang,* about how seemingly opposite forces may actually be complementary, but I didn't really understand it until now.'

'What are you saying? That you're *yin* to his *yang*?'

Jodie shook her head. 'No, actually, the opposite. I'm the stronger of us, which makes me the *yang*. Flynn is receptive, a listener, charming and somewhat easily led. He could do with a strong woman like me.' She looked at her friend, hoping to see a dawning of understanding in her eyes. But her expression was guarded. 'We fit together. Please, wait until you meet him and you'll understand.'

'Fine. I'll reserve judgement.'

'At least you resisted the temptation to say, "don't come crying to me when it all goes pear-shaped",' Jodie said with a grin.

'Only by biting my tongue,' Rivka admitted and returned the smile. 'You're my oldest friend, I don't want to see you hurt.' She reached across the table and held Jodie's hand. 'And yes, I know it's part of life, of relationships, but you're not eighteen anymore, the cut will be deeper, the pain more intense, more long-lasting.'

Jodie pressed the hand that held hers. 'Stop worrying. Some things are worth the risk.'

Jodie went straight home after lunch. It had become second nature now to scan each man's face as she walked down the busy streets and through the bustling train station. Each man in the carriage she sat in was given a once-over as if she were waiting for a little voice somewhere deep in her subconscious to suddenly go, *Aha, that's him.*

And if it did. If she looked across and knew it was Victor... what would she do? Accost him... look him in the eye and remember the childhood he had ended so abruptly... remember the baby she had given away... remember the feeling of love.

She shut her suddenly wet eyes and took a few deep breaths. There was more at stake, more to lose. It took only moments to regain control and she opened eyes that were dry.

Victor wasn't going to destroy what she had now. Whatever it took... she'd make sure of that.

32

It had amused Victor that Jodie had called in the police and he wondered what they'd said. Had they considered the leap from baby shoes to the dead mouse seriously and talked about his 'escalation', worrying her that it could get worse? Or had they dismissed it all as a foolish prank?

His curiosity about Flynn hadn't been completely satisfied by finding out where he lived and learning his name, but there was nothing else to be learned on social media and eventually his interest in the man waned. Flynn was, after all, out of Jodie's life and of no further interest to him.

Jodie was just where Victor wanted her to be – alone and unsettled.

He'd done an internet search and discovered all he needed to know about the NMC investigation. Nothing was going to happen for months. Jodie would be stuck in Gravesend.

It was a good time for him to take a holiday.

Victor had developed a soft spot for Dubai while he was keeping an eye on Jodie and had visited numerous times. The next day, he was on an Emirates flight back.

He lay stretched out on the lounger by the rooftop pool of the same five-star hotel he stayed in every visit, his body toasting to a pale beige. Every hour, almost to the minute, he stood in his badly-fitting swim shorts and dived into the pool. He did ten lengths, frowning at those in the pool who dilly-dallied and got in the way of his smooth breaststroke.

Within a couple of days of his arrival, other visitors, in and out of the pool, had learned to stay out of his way.

Victor didn't notice, his mind was totally occupied with thoughts of Jodie and what he was going to do next.

Two weeks later, Victor packed his bags and took a flight back to London. Although he still hadn't come to any decision about the next step with Jodie, he felt relaxed. He never tanned, but his skin had taken on a faint milky-coffee stain akin to the jaundiced hue of liver complaints.

Back in chilly Gravesend, he opened the door of his bedsit and dropped the small battered suitcase and holdall on the floor. The claustrophobia he always felt after returning from the spacious upmarket hotels he favoured, took a few seconds to fade. Then it was as if he'd never been away, the mugginess of his living space a comfortable familiarity.

He unpacked his few items, threw clothes into the washing machine, and lay down on his bed to shut his eyes after a journey that was more wearisome than usual thanks to delays at every stage. To the hum, rattle and roll of the washing machine he fell asleep.

It was dark when he awoke. Irritation swept over him when he checked the time and discovered it was midnight. He'd wanted to visit Jodie's house, see if he could catch a glimpse of her. He'd have to wait *until the morning and stand in his usual spot. He had seen her go to that other nursing home and guessed it had been for an interview. She was a good nurse, he'd watched her long enough to have come to that conclusion. They would have offered her a job, he was sure of it. She may have already started. He needed to follow her to be certain.*

At 7am, he dressed carefully, layering a long-sleeved T-shirt under his shirt before he slipped on a jumper and finished with his warmest jacket. A scarf around his neck and a beanie hat jammed on his head and he was ready for what could be hours of waiting. He walked the fifteen minutes to the corner of her road, shoved his hands in his pockets and shuffled from foot to foot, his eyes never leaving her front door.

He wasn't kept waiting long. Only ten minutes later, the front door opened and, for a minute, he was fooled. He'd expected to see Jodie, and he assumed the person who came out, wrapped up against the autumnal chill was her. But the form was too big, too wide. And when it turned, when he saw who it was, anger warmed Victor from the inside. He unwrapped the scarf and pulled off his hat as he watched Flynn Douglas walk away.

Rage cleared his mind and twisted his mouth. He knew exactly what he was going to do.

33

Jodie left for work a short while after Flynn. They'd fallen into a routine, getting up at the same time, breakfasting at the table in front of the kitchen window and commenting on the weather outside. He left to get his train, and minutes later, she left for the twenty-five-minute walk to her new job at Seacrest Manor Nursing Home.

It was working out fine for her. It was a busy home, but well-staffed and the management were accommodating. She was only contracted to work twenty-four hours a week in two twelve-hour shifts but she'd worked an extra shift last week and had been asked to work an extra two this week. Most of these extras were at the weekend, a nuisance since Flynn was often off, but she needed to take every opportunity to show the management that she was exactly what she knew herself to be – a good, reliable nurse.

Happy enough at work but glowing at home, Flynn was a dream to live with. They found they had so much in common: music, TV programmes, food, drink. They liked nothing better than to settle down in the evening to watch and dissect their favourite Scandi crime series.

'It's perfect,' she said to Rivka on the phone the end of their first week. 'Now, stop worrying.'

'Fine,' Rivka said, her version of *I'm not sure I believe you but I'm not going to argue*. 'When am I going to meet this paragon of virtue?'

'I never said he was a paragon of anything, simply that we're perfect together. And you'll get to meet him soon. I've been busy with this new job as you know.' In fact, Jodie was putting off a meeting between her friend and Flynn for as long as possible. He was handsome, charming, kind... everything she'd ever wanted in a man... but he wasn't an intellectual and she knew the very clever Rivka would find his conversation a bit lacking.

'Why don't I have you both over for dinner?'

Oh dear, Rivka *and* Tasha. Poor Flynn, she wasn't going to put him through that yet. 'That would be lovely, maybe in a few weeks when everything is more settled.'

'Hmmm, well, okay, if he's still on the scene in a few weeks, we'll have him over.'

That had been a week ago. Jodie was, if anything, more sure she'd made the right decision. She couldn't remember feeling so content... as if she'd been missing something all these years, and Flynn filled that gap.

It turned out that he was a far better cook than she. And more romantic. The first time she'd come home following a twelve-hour shift to find candles lighting, a bottle of her favourite red wine waiting and dinner ready to be served, she started to cry, shocking poor Flynn who stood there blinking in confusion.

She hurried to reassure him that they were tears of happiness, then they sat and ate the delicious food, drank the wine and she thought that life couldn't get any better.

There had been no more packages left on her door and Victor was beginning to fade into the background where he belonged. She'd had a few conversations with her union rep about the NMC investigation, but things were progressing with the speed of a wet week in January. 'It's the way it is,' he told her as if that meant something. 'The longer the better, it gives you time to get some good feedback from your new employer.'

Patience – it wasn't chief among her virtues. She wanted the investigation over, to be able to get on with her life without it darkening the horizon.

That morning, the manager at Seacrest Manor had said he was delighted she'd joined the team. On the advice of her union rep, she asked him to put the comment in writing. Despite the manager's quick assurance that he would, it galled Jodie to have to ask, and she put the nausea that gripped her in the afternoon down to that.

The next morning, when nausea woke her before the alarm, she brushed it off as stress from having to work two twelve-hour shifts back to back. On the third day when nausea disturbed her sleep again, she wondered if she'd caught a bug and lay beside the sleeping Flynn with a hand on her forehead, trying to decide if she had a temperature or not. There was a thermometer in the kitchen drawer, she slipped from the bed, pulled on a robe and tiptoed down the stairs, stopping halfway as her mouth dropped open.

She carried on down but forgot about the search for the thermometer and sat looking out over the garden. The first thing she did every morning – she was religious about it – was to take her contraceptive pill. As soon as one packet finished, she opened the next. She never missed one. Ever... except... her eyes narrowed in thought as she went back to the first night Flynn had stayed over. A smile flickered and died. It had been a wonderful night and the sex had been amazing. She remembered reluctantly dragging herself from bed the following morning to prepare for that awful meeting in the nursing home. And she'd forgotten to take her pill.

It looked as if that one lapse had been enough.

She said nothing to Flynn who bounced down the stairs an hour later full of the joys of the morning. As usual, he brought an instant smile to her lips. 'You're up early,' he said to her, leaning down to plant a kiss on her cheek.

'I woke early, decided to get some coffee and watch the day dawning.' She was frequently a poor sleeper so her comment caused no concern and Flynn busied himself making toast.

He spooned instant coffee into a mug, holding the jar and spoon up as he looked at her. 'You want more coffee?'

'No, thanks, I've already had a mug.' The nausea had faded but she didn't want to risk it returning and having to explain... or lie. If she was right, she wanted time to adjust to the thought before she told him. Once the words were out, there'd be no going back.

'Any plans for the day,' Flynn asked, taking the seat opposite. Toast crumbs fell from the slice he was eating in huge bites. Dinner was for dilly-dallying, he'd once told her when she'd commented that he finished each slice in four bites. Breakfast, on the other hand, he'd explained, was for getting fuel inside as quickly as possible.

Nausea rolled as she watched him. She gulped and looked away. 'I need to do some shopping this morning, then I plan to have a lazy afternoon. The new crime thriller by Jenny O'Brien I ordered last week popped up on my Kindle this morning, so I fancy curling up on the sofa for a few hours and getting lost in that.'

'Good, you need to rest after those two long days.' Flynn drained his coffee, got to his feet and checked the time. 'Better get going. I should be home around six.' He put his plate and mug in the dishwasher and reached for his coat, pulling it on as he leaned in again to give her a kiss, this time a lingering one on her lips.

Jodie reached a hand up and lay it on his cheek. 'Don't work too hard. I'll have dinner ready when you get home. I might surprise you and do something special.' She laughed and whacked him across the arm when he mimed vomiting. 'Cheeky! I can cook.'

'Of course you can.' He grinned. 'I might get a McDonald's on the way home all the same.'

He was still laughing at his own joke as he walked down the street, turning every few steps to look back and wave at her as she stood in the doorway, waving him off.

Her smile faded as she returned to the kitchen. The nausea had completely subsided so she made a slice of toast and a mug of coffee and sat looking out at the garden. Garden... it was a yard, only a few feet across. Not enough space for a child to play.

A child! Her second chance. A brother... or sister... for the man who was probably strolling on Bondi beach, maybe with his girlfriend... maybe with his own child. The thought tugged at her heart. All she'd missed out on.

She put her coffee down and rubbed her hands over her belly. If, as she'd guessed, it had happened that night, it was a little over four weeks ago. Early days. Anything could happen. Her hands rested on her flat stomach. No. Nothing was going to happen. She was going to have this baby. A child with a man she loved. A second chance. She deserved it.

She wanted it.

34

Victor had only been gone two weeks and Jodie had changed everything. It took him over a week to establish for certain that Flynn was living full-time with her. She'd let him into her home... and into her bed.

It was time she realised that he wasn't the man for her. Victor's thin lips twisted in a sneer. He was lying in his favourite thinking place, stretched out on the bed, hands clasped behind his head. He was done with hanging stuff on her door – it was time to confront Jodie, to tell her what he was sure she knew in her heart.

Her happy little world was built on a lie. The cosy walks to the nearby restaurant hand in hand, the intimate nights when they locked the door behind themselves and never came out again, leaving Victor to imagine what was going on inside. Sometimes, he'd stroll by, slowing as he passed her door, his ears pricked to listen. The odd time she'd have left her curtains open and he'd be able to catch a sign of the life that was going on inside. He'd take out his mobile and pretend to talk into it as he peered through her window. Once he imagined that he heard laughter... and another time he was convinced he could hear the grunts and groans of lust.

Victor sneered at the memory. He swung his feet to the ground, reached under the bed and pulled out a dusty, battered briefcase. It took a bit of jiggling before the clasp gave way and the lid flew open sending a cloud of dust into the air that had Victor bent double with a wet, phlegmy cough. A minute later, he wiped the tears from his brown eyes and blew his nose with the corner of his grubby sheet. The briefcase was filled with a jumble of papers. His bony fingers scrabbled until they found what he wanted – a sheet of writing paper and an envelope.

What to write? He sat for a long time at the table, waiting for inspiration. It was important to get it right. The words couldn't be frightening or threatening – otherwise Jodie might go straight to the police. He had to lie and reassure her that he meant no harm. The words had to be tantalising, so she wouldn't simply dismiss them. He needed her to agree to meet. He wanted, desperately, to see the look on her face when he told her.

He tapped the pen he held against the cheap pine table and stared at the blank page until his eyes grew tired. Maybe in the morning, when he was fresh, the right words would come.

At 2am, Victor woke from a strange dream that faded as he reached for it. Whatever it had been, it had chased sleep away. He switched on the light and sat up. The blank sheet of paper was glaring white under the neon strip lighting. Naked, he sat on the chair and picked up the pen. In the end, it was simple.

Jodie,
There is something you need to know.
Victor

He added his address to the top of the page, then read over it, grimacing in satisfaction. That would do very well indeed. He folded the sheet and shoved it into the envelope.

Flynn, he'd noted, always left the house by 7.15am. He'd wait till after and post it through her letterbox.

Victor extended the tip of his coated tongue, licked the envelope and thought of Jodie.

35

Jodie sat for another twenty minutes before getting to her feet. There was a pharmacy not far away, she'd go at nine and get a pregnancy test. As soon as she knew for sure, she could make plans to tell Flynn. This early in their relationship, having children hadn't come up in conversation. Would he be happy? Or shocked?

Happy, she guessed. She could imagine him with children, a big goofy grin on his face.

In the hallway, the envelope on the floor by the front door caught her by surprise. It was too early for the post to have come. She leaned down to pick it up, stopping when she was within touching distance. Suddenly, with total certainty, she knew who it was from. A few steps backward took her to the stairway. She sat heavily on the second step and stared at the innocent-looking white envelope.

There'd be something less innocent inside. Not a dead mouse this time. But words could be more horrific, more wounding.

She was trembling as she stood, her hand shaking as she bent to pick it up. It was easier to sit back down on the stair while she opened it, her legs didn't seem capable of going further. The flap of the envelope wasn't completely stuck down. She slipped her finger under the opening and slid it across.

Inside, there was a folded sheet of paper. She removed it, dropped the envelope and opened the page out. It was short. To the point. Victor wanted to tell her something. Something she needed to know. Irritatingly, it was that vague. Something! But what?

He hadn't asked to meet her anywhere but his address was written boldly across the top of the page. His address – she was shocked but not surprised to see that he lived only a short walk from her house. Did he expect her to call on him? Was he absolutely crazy? Or did he think she was?

She picked up the envelope, took it and the note to the kitchen and pushed them down into the rubbish bin. With the hot tap running, she squirted soap into her hands and scrubbed them, waiting until the water ran scalding hot to rinse it off.

Her nausea this time had little to do with the child she might or might not be carrying. *Victor.* What could he possibly want to tell her?

The reason he'd sent her those packages. That had to be it.

Or maybe not.

Victor, she knew had been watching her house. He would know about Flynn. Maybe he knew all about him – about his silly impersonation – and simply wanted to warn her about a lie she already knew.

But what if it were something else?

After all, the little voice inside her head whispered, Flynn had lied to her before. Maybe Victor knew something else about him.

She had no choice but to go to Victor's and find out. And there was no point in putting it off. She'd go immediately. Her hands slipped over her stomach again. Afterwards, she'd go to the pharmacy, buy a pregnancy test and confirm what she knew.

Fifteen minutes later, Jodie was dressed in jeans, a dark flannel shirt she rarely wore and her walking shoes for comfort and speed. She had no idea what she was going to face, it was better to be prepared. Her hair was loose, bouncing around her face in waves. She grabbed it in her hand and tied it back with a band.

The addition of a heavy, shapeless, navy coat and she was satisfied. She looked tough, severe, sexless. Ready to face whatever it was that was going to be thrown at her.

She grabbed her house keys and left.

It wasn't far to where Victor lived. Jodie walked briskly, long strides beating the path to the address he'd given her; a dilapidated house, in a row of the same. Each was fronted by a tiny overgrown garden, the only colour among the weeds coming from discarded beer cans and plastic wrappers that would never decompose.

Doorbells were set in the wooden frame to the right of the door. Twelve of them, strangely set one atop the other and all identified by a faded letter rather than a name. Jodie's finger hovered over the H, then pressed quickly.

If the bell was ringing inside, it wasn't audible from where she stood, her lip curling as she took in the shabby, unkempt premises. The bottom-right corner of the wooden front door had rot, leaving a hole she was sure mice could easily get through. She remembered the mouse Victor had sent her and shivered.

The thought sent anger darting through her. She put her finger to the bell and pressed again, keeping it there for several seconds. The pathway was narrow, the road busy but she stepped back as far as she could and looked up to the windows above. There was no sign anyone was staring down, no curtain twitching, no face appearing.

She'd almost decided to leave when the door opened inward, wood scraping against the tiled floor, a sound beloved of horror movies that would have made her laugh if the circumstances weren't so... bloody terrifying. She took a deep breath on that thought and let it out slowly, reminding herself, yet again, she was no longer fourteen.

Her breath caught. The man who stood there, one hand on the door, the other raised palm outward in a static wave, looked old and frail, his jaundiced skin telling Jodie, the nurse, that there might be something seriously wrong with him.

She had anticipated not recognising Victor but there'd been a part of her that had thought she'd see something of the young man she'd adored in the man he had become. And there was nothing. She wasn't even one hundred per cent sure that it was Victor standing there.

'It's been a long time, Jodie.' His lips parted in the semblance of a smile. 'What? You don't recognise me? Prison tends to have that effect, my dear. The daily fear wears you down and ages you.'

'How do I know–'

'That I'm Victor?' His smile broadened. 'I suppose you're going to have to trust me.'

Jodie looked up and down the street. This was a bad idea. If she chose to go in, wasn't she putting herself in a very precarious position. Victor looked old and frail, but maybe it was an act he was putting on. Her eyes narrowed, that peculiar hue to his skin though, that didn't augur well.

When Victor stood back and waved her in, she took a final look around and stepped inside.

The door slammed behind her, her yelp of shock an automatic response. She turned and glared at him. A single bare bulb hung from the high ceiling of the narrow hallway. It provided little illumination, creating unsettling shades and shadows, and leaving the corners, where anything could be hiding, in complete darkness. Even in the poor light, she could see Victor's gleeful smile at her discomfort.

'Sorry. The door is rotten, it's hard to shut.' He indicated the stairway behind. 'I'm on the third floor. No lift, I'm afraid.'

Jodie followed his slow ascent, trying not to breathe too deeply. There was a pervasive smell of damp and rot but there were others, more subtle but equally noisome, that made her stomach flip-flop. She needed something positive to cling to. After this, she'd confirm what she knew, and start planning for her future.

On the third floor, Victor pushed open a fire door. 'Almost there.'

At the end of a narrow corridor, he stopped. 'Ta-dah!' He grinned, opened the door, and waited for her to step through.

The line of a poem she'd learned as a child popped unexpectedly into Jodie's head. *'Come into my parlour,' said the spider to the fly.* She could remember no more, couldn't remember the fate of the poor fly, and felt foolishly grateful she didn't.

She'd liked to have been able to say 'very nice' or something somewhat appreciative of the space she found herself in but there was nothing she could say about the poky bedsit. A single bed stretched across one wall, a cheap pine table and a single chair filling the space between it and the tiny kitchen. Pity swept over her, unbidden, she didn't want to feel sorry for him but the one chair told a sad tale of lonely meals for one.

Apart from the entrance, there was only one other door – she assumed it led to an equally small bathroom.

'Have a seat.' Victor pointed to the chair. 'Would you like a drink? I have a very nice whisky.'

The metal chair squeaked as she sat on the edge, tension keeping her upright. 'This isn't a social call, Victor. Tell me what you want to tell me and I'll be on my way.' It took effort to keep the tremble from her voice, her words coming out harsh and cold as a result.

'No ramble down memory lane then,' he said. He perched on the side of the bed. 'As you wish.' He stared at her silently. 'You've barely changed, my dear. You still look as beautiful as you did when we were... together.'

Jodie shivered at the hint of lust in his words and looked towards the door. Nobody knew where she was. This had been one of her worst ideas. She took a nervous step towards it, her head jerking back when Victor got to his feet.

'Am I making you uneasy?' he asked with a twist of his mouth. 'I never used to.'

She stepped back, folded her arms, and looked at him coldly. 'That was a long time ago. I was a child, easily swayed.' She watched as he dragged a scruffy case from under the bed.

'I kept it safe for you,' Victor said, sitting back on the bed. 'It wouldn't do if my proof went missing, would it?' He kept his eyes on her as he opened the case, each clasp releasing with a loud snap. His grin grew wider and it was clear to Jodie he was relishing the drama of it all, enjoying her undivided attention... the way he always used to.

She was fixated by the battered case and fascinated by his long fingers as they opened it. He was watching her, as she was watching him, a weird tableau out of time.

Victor reached into the case without taking his eyes from her. 'Here it is.' He pulled out a small photograph. 'Are you sure you want to see it?'

Of course, she didn't... and did. 'I'm not playing games, Victor. If there's something you want to tell me and to show me, then get on with it. Otherwise I'm leaving.'

'Fair enough.' He got to his feet and took a step towards her.

The room was small, stuffy. He was close enough that she could smell him, an unpleasant odour of unwashed clothes and poor personal hygiene that made her press her lips together and screw up her nose. She resisted the temptation to move away and held out her hand for the photograph he continued to wave.

He took a final look at it, then put it into her hand and stepped back to resume his perch on the bed.

Jodie waited a beat before looking at the photograph. She hadn't known what to expect so was mildly surprised to see it was nothing more ominous than a photograph of her and Victor.

The fourteen-year-old Jodie looked happy, a wide smile on her young, smooth cheeks, her hair hanging loose around her shoulders. Victor's arm was draped around her waist, and he was looking down into her face as she looked adoringly up at him. She had been so young, so innocent. Jodie's fingers tightened on the photograph. It was a long time ago. 'I don't understand.' She frowned and looked at Victor sitting on the edge of the bed like a goblin, an expectant smile on his lips. 'Why are you showing this to me?'

His smile grew and he pointed to the photograph. 'Don't tell me you don't see it, Jodie. Look at the love that is shining between us. It's never faded, not in all the years. We loved one another then, we still love one another.'

Jodie dropped the photograph as if it had burned her, a half-laugh of disbelief, half-cry of despair escaping from her clenched lips. 'You're mad,' she said, backing away.

36

Victor bent and picked up the discarded photo. 'You know I'm right. That man, that Flynn is just a boy. You need an older man, you always did.'

He watched as Jodie tried to fight the truth. She'd understand eventually, the same way he did. It was why he'd never been able to let her go, why he'd followed her for years.

'You're mad,' Jodie said again, shaking her head. 'I was only a child, a vulnerable child, you groomed me, manipulated me.'

Victor smiled at her. 'You know that's not the truth. You were brainwashed by your mother, by social services. They didn't understand. Think about it... you've never married, never had a long-term committed relationship, have you?' His smile grew as he saw the truth in her eyes. He could read her as easily today as he could all those years ago. 'You see, you know I'm right. You love me.'

He saw her confusion, understood it. Hadn't he misunderstood for years, hate and love... such close emotions, he'd confused them but now it was clear... it would be clear for her too... soon... he wouldn't stop until she understood... he'd keep trying to persuade her.

They were meant for each other.

37

A shaky step took Jodie nearer the door. 'The only emotion I feel for you is pity. You're deluded. Sick. You're sick, Victor.'

He got to his feet and moved towards her. 'I haven't aged well, I give you that, but when I was younger, you adored me, swooned when I touched you.' When he reached a hand for her, she stumbled backward, her mouth twisting in disgust.

The tip of Victor's tongue appeared and slid from one corner of his mouth to the other.

Jodie shook her head. This couldn't be happening. How stupid she had been to come here. Feeling the room spin, she reached for the door handle. She had to get out of there.

But Victor, as she'd suspected, could move fast when he wanted to and she felt her arm caught in a grip that shocked her with its strength as he pulled her into his embrace. She'd been wrong, this close to him there was no sign of illness, his skin colour might be odd but there was no yellow in the white of his eyes. She'd been fooled. Or maybe she'd simply seen what she'd wanted to see.

'You know I'm right, Jodie,' Victor said, his fingers tightening on her arm, hurting. 'You love me, I know you do.'

Jodie was almost overcome with the smell that came from him with every word, a foul stink that made her weak. She reached down for every atom of strength she had and lifted her chin. This close, she could see flecks of green in the brown eyes that were boring into hers and fought to meet them without wavering. *Show no fear, it was the way to fight monsters.* 'I was smitten with you when I was a child, a vulnerable child who'd lost her father the year before and was easy game for a manipulative sleazebag.'

Victor's face moved closer, his lips parting. Jodie was horrified and nauseated to see the raw meat gloss of his tongue. She would rather die... or fight. She drew her free arm back and drove the heel of her hand into his chest with as much strength as she could gather. The force of the blow, or perhaps the surprise of it, worked, and Victor released her arm, stumbled backwards and fell to the floor.

Jodie wanted to hit him again, wanted to keep on doing so, wanted to shout and scream, kick him, stamp on him, let the anger she hadn't realised she had stored for all those years to erupt in one huge volcanic explosion. She took a step towards him, then took two steps back, all anger suddenly dissipating.

'I was a child,' she said, and felt the release of those lingering hints of guilt that she was somehow to blame. 'A very young fourteen-year-old. And you took horrendous advantage of my innocence, my youth, my vulnerability.' She stepped closer again, her lip curling in a sneer when she saw fear creep across his face. 'You are a monster, Victor, worse, a craven monster who preys on the weak and defenceless. That was why you sent me those packages before your declaration of–' she lifted her index fingers to make quotation marks in the air '–love. You wanted me weak, scared, anxious.'

She used the toe of her shoe to prod his leg. 'But I'm none of those things.' A few steps backward took her to the door. She reached for the handle without taking her eyes from him. 'I'm going. I don't want to see you again. If I do, if I even see you in the distance, I'll go to the police and complain that you're stalking me.'

Without another word, she opened the door and hurried down the corridor. She took the stairs two steps at a time, almost tripping over herself in her haste to leave.

By the time she reached home, she was shaking from a combination of anger, relief, and disgust. Her fingers fumbled with the house key, panic in every breath. Inside, she slammed the door behind her, reached for the safety chain and slid it into place. Only then did she feel safe. It was an hour before she calmed down, an hour she spent stomping around the house unable to settle to doing anything.

Victor... he was a delusional monster. She had considered that he might still love her after all these years, crazy though that notion was. What she'd never considered, was that he might think she felt the same. The idea made her squirm.

If she saw him, even once, she'd go straight to the police. Any pity for him had been wiped away by his declaration. Victor may no longer be on the sex offenders register but he was still an ex-con, if she told the police he was stalking her and that he'd been the one responsible for the packages, they'd have to take her seriously.

Hours later, by concentrating on the memory of Victor as she'd left him, a seedy, pathetic man lying on the floor, Jodie was almost able to forget that he was a monster. She'd shown him that she wasn't the pushover she'd been as a child. Perhaps he'd leave her alone now.

With that hope lodged firmly in her brain, she decided to go to the pharmacy as planned. Her hands sneaked over her flat belly as if to comfort what was growing inside. She wasn't going to live her life in fear, and she was desperate to confirm what she suspected.

∼

The pharmacy, part of a chain, was big and busy. It wasn't somewhere she normally shopped and she'd no idea where to locate what she wanted. Unwilling to ask the heavily made-up young woman who was straightening a display of luridly coloured nail varnish, Jodie wandered up and down the aisles until she found what she was looking for.

Twenty minutes later, she was back at home reading the instructions and a mere five minutes after that, she was squealing with joy. She'd known she was right, but looking at the confirmation in her hand, she couldn't help a grin of pleasure. This time it was perfect. She was going to have a child with a man she loved.

Her second chance.

Nothing was going to mess this up.

38

Excited though she was, Jodie didn't tell Flynn that evening, or the next. It was too early both in terms of their relationship and in the pregnancy. This early she could easily lose the baby. This early, their relationship might yet founder.

For the moment, she kept her exciting news to herself.

Over the next few days, she watched for Victor's face in the crowd. But if he were there, he was staying well hidden. It didn't stop Jodie searching, her eyes darting left and right as she walked on a busy street or through the train station.

Five days after she'd called to his bedsit, she began to hope that that particular nightmare was over.

It was the sixth day, a day when she wasn't working, that she came down shortly after Flynn had left to find an envelope on the hall mat. She didn't have to pick it up to know who it was from and a jolt of anger shot through her. Victor had lulled her into thinking she'd won, that he'd run away with his tail between his legs but it was obviously part of his plan to unsettle and weaken her.

She'd warned him, hadn't she?

Her mobile was beside her bed, she turned to go back up for it. She'd ring the police. Get them to do their job.

Halfway up, she gave a grunt of frustration and returned to the hallway. The police would want to know everything. She'd have to tell them she'd visited his bedsit. How would they view that? Visiting the bedsit of a man she'd accused of statutory rape all those years ago. They'd think it a bit strange. Hell, she thought it a bit strange. What had she been thinking?

She scooped the letter up and took it with her to the kitchen, leaving it on the table while she made coffee.

Nausea rumbled as it did every morning. Usually, by ten, it had settled down and, so far, she'd been lucky, it hadn't prevented her from working. She sipped her coffee, her eyes fixed on the envelope. As with the last, her name was scrawled in spidery writing across the front. And inside... what would it be this time?

A spurt of anger made her reach for it, tear it open across the top and knock the contents onto the table. A folded sheet of paper and a small photograph. They didn't look threatening.

Not threatening but Victor's missive wasn't subtle.

I love you, I've always loved you.

Jodie crushed the paper in her hand and flung it across the room before picking up the photograph. It was the one he'd shown her, the two of them. They looked happy, so at ease. How well he had groomed her, to have made her think it was all normal.

She held the photograph up to the light and peered closer at Victor. He'd been twenty-eight when they'd met. Over the years, history had shaded his face in unfriendly colours so she'd forgotten how handsome he'd been. She'd deliberately tried to forget about him, about the disgrace, the pain, the loss.

He was trying to rekindle something that had never existed. She had to find a way to stop him.

39

Jodie tore the photograph and note into tiny pieces and threw them into the rubbish bin. If only she could dispense with Victor so easily.

At noon, she left the house and headed into the city to meet Rivka for lunch. She'd not met her in a couple of weeks, making excuses when her friend rang, afraid she'd blurt out the news of the pregnancy in her excitement and happiness. She wanted to wait until those first three months of uncertainty were up.

Uncertainty. Her life seemed to be filled with it.

In the café, she ordered a coffee while she waited, raising a hand in greeting when her friend arrived on the dot of one. Jodie blinked in surprise to see her normally bright-eyed and cheerful friend looking pale and unusually solemn. 'You look frazzled,' she said as Rivka sat on the chair opposite. 'Are you okay?'

Rather than answering, Rivka leaned forward, her eyes fixed on the table in front of her. 'How is the NMC investigation going?'

Jodie tried to read her friend's expression, but it was shut down, her skin unusually pale, lips a thin red slash. Maybe she'd had a row with Tasha? 'Is everything okay?'

'The investigation. Tell me.'

Jodie had already decided against telling Rivka about her visit to Victor's. It had been a crazy thing to do, she wanted to forget about it and certainly didn't want to listen to Rivka's justifiable criticism. It was unusual for her friend to be so odd but if she wanted to talk about the NMC investigation, Jodie would humour her. 'There's not much to tell. I've had letters and forms to fill out but that's it. I was warned that it would take a long time. My union rep seems happy enough, he says it gives me time to get good character references from my new employer.'

'But it will eventually be dismissed?'

Rivka's hands were clasped on the table, tension in every line of her body. Unusually, too, for the normally well-turned-out woman, she wasn't wearing any makeup, and her hair looked as though it hadn't been washed in a couple of days. Everything screamed something was wrong. Jodie stretched a hand across the table. 'Hey, what's the matter?'

Rivka looked at the hand, but instead of reaching for it, she shoved her hands into her coat pockets and repeated her question. 'It will eventually be dismissed?'

Jodie left her hand where it was as she answered. 'I've no idea. I've never put a foot wrong before so that's in my favour. The home can't prove it was me who left the medication in the room but the NMC may come to the same conclusion that the home did and lay the blame squarely on my shoulders.'

'Then you could still be struck off?'

'Yes, I suppose I could.' Jodie shrugged. 'I'm hoping not, obviously.' She tapped the table gently with her extended hand. 'Are you going to tell me what's wrong?'

Rivka lifted her chin and looked at her with tear-filled eyes.

In all the years Jodie had known her, she'd never seen her look so utterly sad. 'Rivka, what the hell is going on?'

'If you had a letter from the person who put the tablets in that resident's bedroom, would that exonerate you completely?'

So many things had bowled Jodie over in the last few weeks, she should be used to the sensation of falling into a deep pit. But this was Rivka. Her rock in an increasingly unstable world. Unable to formulate a rational question Jodie fell back on, 'I don't understand.'

Rivka pulled her hands from her pockets. One held a rather battered, creased envelope. 'Here.'

Another damn white envelope. Jodie had had her fill of them. She shook her head, knowing by her friend's grim expression that the contents were going to shake her. But she wasn't being given a choice. Rivka pushed the envelope into Jodie's hand and sat back, her chin on her chest.

The envelope wasn't sealed. Jodie pulled out a folded sheet of writing paper and with a glance towards Rivka, unfolded it and read. It was short. Blunt. And shocking.

To whom it may concern.

I, Tasha White, do confess that on the 16th September I entered the BestLife Care Home in Gravesend and planted medication in room six in order to incriminate Jodie Armstrong. I apologise for the trouble and hurt I have caused.

Tasha White

'Tasha?' Jodie looked up from the letter. 'I don't believe it! Why would she have done such a thing?' When Rivka remained silent, Jodie stretched a hand across, grabbed her arm and shook it. 'Talk to me!'

Rivka lifted her head. 'It was my fault,' she said quietly. 'I knew Tasha was jealous of our friendship but I hadn't realised how often I spoke of you, and how often I mentioned what a good nurse you are, how professional, efficient and so on.' Rivka rubbed her hands over her face. 'She's not a nurse so she'd no idea of the implications. She simply thought you'd get into trouble and your halo would be slightly tarnished.'

'How?' Jodie was having trouble taking it in. *Tasha?*

'It was ridiculously easy. She pinched some tablets from my mother's supply the last time we visited her. I had your work rota pinned to the noticeboard so she was able to choose a day you were working–'

'And simply walked in!'

Rivka nodded. 'She said she hung around outside until she saw a group of visitors going in and attached herself to them. Once inside, she scurried along a corridor, went into the first open door and left the tablets on a bedside locker.'

Jodie was struggling to make sense of it all. 'They were found in a medicine pot. Where would she have got her hands on one?'

A flash of red coloured Rivka's pale cheeks. 'I sometimes take them home from the clinic in my uniform pocket and forget to bring them back. It was easy for her to keep one.'

Jodie had never taken to Tasha, and she'd guessed the feeling was mutual. But this! She planned it all to make Jodie look bad. 'It's unbelievable.' It explained the state of her friend. 'How did you find out?'

'She's been a bit irritable recently and I wondered if she was having second thoughts about us. So last night I asked her.'

'And she confessed?'

'Yes.' Rivka pointed to the letter that lay on the table between them. 'It was her idea to write that. She is terribly sorry and wants to make amends.' She waited a beat. 'What are you going to do?'

'I'll give the letter to my union rep. He'll take it to the NMC and hopefully they'll decide I have no case to answer.' Jodie tapped the letter. 'They'll probably tell the nursing home but I doubt if they will pursue it, after all, it doesn't reflect well on BestLife Care that someone can simply sail in and leave medication around willy-nilly.'

Rivka looked relieved and wiped a hand over her face. 'That's what I thought.'

Jodie frowned as the truth dawned. 'You're going to stay with her.' She picked up the letter and waved it. 'Despite this? How can you bear to stay with a woman who would do such a thing?'

'I love her,' Rivka said. 'I'd probably forgive her anything.' She dropped her gaze to the table again.

Suddenly, Jodie knew there was worse to come. 'What are you not telling me?'

Rivka didn't lift her head. 'I love Tasha, and I'd do anything for her.' She looked up then, and a tear trickled down her cheek. 'Even give up my friendship with you.'

Jodie barked a laugh. This had to be a joke! She and Rivka had been friends for ever. Since their student nurse days. Almost twenty years. 'You can't be serious.'

'I'm sorry. Maybe in a few months we can reconnect, you know, when Tasha understands that she is the most important thing in my life.'

Jodie thought about all the scrapes they'd been in together. The hours they'd spent laughing, talking and growing up, the secrets and lies they'd shared.

Maybe they were all grown up at last.

The letter sat on the table between them. Jodie took it, folded it, put it into her pocket and got to her feet. 'I hope it all works out for you, Rivka.' Jodie turned and left the café.

40

J odie wanted to wail and gnash her teeth, get very drunk, go around to Rivka and Tasha's apartment and smash Tasha in the face with her fist. But she did none of these things. She'd promised to cook dinner, and that's what she was going to do. She shopped for the easiest meal she could think to make, the loss of her friend, and of their years of friendship, weighing her down with every step she took through the supermarket as she tossed items inside willy-nilly.

'Very nice,' Flynn said that evening, cutting into fillet steak.

Jodie had given herself the smaller fillet and less of the roasted vegetables. She pushed the food around the plate taking miniscule pieces and swallowing them almost unchewed. She'd filled her wine glass and left it undrunk. It was easier. Flynn, she knew, wouldn't notice that she wasn't drinking and she wouldn't have to lie.

Lie. She'd been so horrified at Flynn's deception and it shocked her that she was willing to lie rather than tell the truth about the pregnancy. It was too soon, that was what she kept telling herself, but was that it really? Or was she afraid he'd baulk at the thought of their having a baby?

She nodded in reply to a question Flynn asked, his face animated, eyes sparkling. She loved him. The thought rocked her. She loved him. And she'd do anything for him.

The anger she felt towards Rivka faded to a deep sadness. Jodie understood. She'd do anything now to keep Flynn by her side.

A wave of nausea hit her and she dropped her fork, shaking her head and forcing a smile when Flynn stopped speaking and looked at her with concern. 'You okay?'

'Yes, sorry, I had lunch with Rivka earlier, I think I ate something that didn't agree with me.'

'You're not finishing that?' Flynn waved a fork at the meat she'd barely touched and when she shook her head, he speared it with a grin. 'More for me.'

'I might not see Rivka for a while actually,' she said, feeling the raw sting of the words as she said them. 'It seems Tasha is jealous of me.'

'Really? But you and Rivka have been friends for years, haven't you?'

'Yes, but it's all come to a head.' She took a sip of her wine, wishing she could knock back the glass. 'The medication that was left in the nursing home...' She waited to get Flynn's full attention before continuing. 'It was Tasha. She confessed. She wanted to get me into trouble. To tarnish my halo, Rivka said. Not fired,' she added quickly, as if that made all the difference.

Flynn raised an eyebrow. 'Wow! That must have come as a shock.'

'A bit.' Jodie remembered Rivka's sad face and reached for the wine. Her fingers played with the stem but she didn't lift the glass.

Flynn was working his way through her piece of steak and didn't appear to notice. 'You'll be able to get the case against you dropped, won't you? Maybe get your old job back.'

'Probably yes, and definitely no,' she said. 'I couldn't go back there. Anyway, I'm fine where I am.' She filled his wine glass and sat back in her chair. 'Let's talk about something more cheerful. I was thinking that maybe next summer we could go on a nice holiday.'

'Mmm,' he mumbled through a mouthful of food. 'Devon maybe?'

She smiled. 'I was thinking of further than that.'

'Abroad?' He stopped chewing and looked at her with wide eyes as if *abroad* was an alien concept.

'Yes. Don't you like to travel?'

He shook his head slowly. 'In the UK, yes, but I've never been outside. Don't see the point really. There's so much to see here.'

Shock silenced her. He'd never been outside the UK? How had she not known this about him. *Because you barely know him*, a little voice whispered in glee. 'Don't you want to go to Italy, France or Spain even?'

He stopped with the fork halfway to his mouth. 'No, I've seen it in the movies.'

There wasn't much to say to that. She'd seen Venice, Florence, Paris, even Amsterdam in movies... there was little comparison to the reality of walking through them, of lingering over coffee in one of their magnificent squares and watching the world go by. 'You do have a passport, though, don't you?'

'Sure.' He shrugged. 'I got it when a few mates were talking about going to Benidorm last year. In the end nothing came of it. Suited me. We stayed in the UK.'

But Jodie loved to travel. She'd pictured the two... three of them... exploring the world together.

Then Flynn smiled at her and reached across to take her hand in his big warm one and she melted. She was being an idiot. So, he didn't fancy travelling. She loved him. She'd love him in Devon. Hell, she'd love him no matter where he wanted to go.

Later, curled up on the sofa, her head nestled into his shoulder and her hand resting on her belly, she thought of Rivka. It wouldn't have been easy for her friend to do what she'd done, to give up their friendship for love. Then Victor's seedy face appeared in her head.

He'd not given up his campaign, the letter and photograph had proved that. What could she do to make him understand? Flynn laughed at something on the TV. She looked up at him and smiled, the smile fading as she realised that, like Rivka, she'd do whatever was necessary.

41

Flynn had given up his share of the flat and moved all his belongings into Jodie's house. They'd laughed as they tried to fit all his clothes into the wardrobes and the single drawer that Jodie offered him.

'We'll have to get more furniture,' Jodie said, squashing his underwear down with a hand and pushing the drawer shut. 'Maybe we could have a look in the shops at the weekend?'

They had and eventually, after three shops and much opening and shutting of doors, they'd purchased another wardrobe.

It was being delivered that day. Between ten and two they'd promised but it was five past the later hour when the doorbell finally rang. Jodie had been waiting impatiently, drinking water and lazily flicking through a catalogue that had landed on her mat that morning.

The delivery men were pleasant, apologetic for being late, and quite happy to bring the wardrobe up the stairs when asked. It came in two pieces for easy transport, an upper part for hanging clothes and a lower part with drawers. Within a few minutes, they had it in position and joined together.

Jodie checked her watch. She wanted to surprise Flynn by having all his belongings neatly put away by the time he arrived home. That gave her a little over two hours. No problem.

Most of his suits, on hangers, had been left lying on the spare bed. By the time they were hanging up there wasn't a lot of space left on the rail but there were still the drawers below to fill. She took the clothes that had been jammed into the drawer of the dresser in handfuls and put them into the lower drawer. She was removing the last few items when she came upon a small plastic wallet and, naturally curious, opened it. She wasn't expecting to find anything exciting: there were some credit card statements, a dental appointment card that made her smile, and right at the back, Flynn's passport.

She still couldn't believe he'd never used it and shook her head before pulling it out and flicking it open. Unsurprisingly, he took a good photo. Brown eyes looking straight into the camera, his expression serious, a hint of a smile lurking out of sight.

Then she read the rest.

The urge to vomit came suddenly. She dropped the passport, the wallet and the last items of clothing and rushed to the bathroom where she dry-retched, finally bringing up the small amount of water she'd drunk.

She slipped down to the bathroom floor, rested back against the side of the bath, and wiped a hand over her mouth.

It wasn't possible. Flynn swore he'd never lie to her again. Yet there it was in a legal document, proof that he had. In the café, a lifetime ago, he'd said he was twenty-eight, the passport said he was twenty-four.

But unlike men, passports didn't lie.

She was stunned into immobility by the ramifications of what she'd discovered, and was still sitting on the bathroom floor in the dim light of early evening when she heard the key in the door. It was followed by the double clunk as Flynn took one shoe off, then the other, dropping them in the corner of the hallway. He'd assume she'd be in the kitchen.

'Jodie, where are you? Did it come? Oh wow, that's fab.'

There was the creak of doors and the rattle of hangers before he called again. 'Jodie?'

'I'm here.' Her voice was lost, just like her. 'Here.' A little louder, enough to bring him to the doorway, concern etching his face to see her sitting there.

'What's the matter?' He reached her, hunkered down, and held a hand against her face. 'Did you fall? Are you hurt?'

'How old are you, Flynn?'

'How old am I?' He took his hand away and got to his feet. 'Seriously, you're sitting on the bathroom floor wondering how old I am? What difference does it make?'

Her stomach flip-flopped. 'You lied.'

It wouldn't have been a problem if he had been the only one who had lied.

No, the problem was that so had she.

Flynn sat on the floor beside her, reached across and grabbed her hand, keeping it in his as she tried to pull away. 'That day in the café, you looked so sweet. I think I fell in love with you that minute. There was something about you that appealed to me. And when we talked, it was so easy. And you were willing to lose it for the sake of a few years, I knew you were, so I added a few on.'

'Four,' she said, feeling the earth crack beneath her. 'You added four years on to make you twenty-eight.'

'My mother used to call them social lies, they're never meant to harm anyone.' He leaned forward to look at her. 'There's no harm done: so you're ten years older than me, not six, does it really matter?'

'Fourteen,' she said, and the crack under her grew wider. 'I'm fourteen years older than you because, yes, I was conscious of the age difference so I dropped a few years. I didn't think it would matter... I really didn't think it would.'

'It doesn't matter,' he said, reaching for her other hand. 'Six, ten, fourteen years between us. So what? I don't care. I love you, I've never felt like this about anyone before.'

Jodie pulled her hands away and struggled to her feet, brushing him away when he tried to help. 'You don't understand, Flynn.' He didn't, because she'd lied to him from the very beginning. And now it looked as if she was going to pay.

She heard him sigh and follow her down the stairs. She'd have liked a drink, she'd have liked to get steaming drunk and not sober up for a long, long time. But she couldn't. She was pregnant. A cry escaped, startling her and Flynn who was a step behind.

'For goodness' sake, Jodie, what's going on?'

'You weren't the only one who was lying about who you were,' she said, her voice tight and barely above a whisper. 'Your impersonation was more obvious and oddly, more honest, than mine.' She saw his puzzled look. 'I lied to you. About the child I had.'

Flynn sat on the seat opposite and stretched a hand across the table. 'It doesn't matter.'

Instead of taking his hand, she folded her arms across her chest. 'How can you possibly know that it doesn't?'

'I know I love you, and you love me. Isn't that all that matters?'

'No, not in this case.' She looked away, unable to bear seeing the hurt in his eyes when she told him the truth. 'I led you to believe I had the child after my mother died, but I didn't, I had him long before that.' The chair rattled as she got to her feet. 'Hang on a sec,' she said and left him to run upstairs.

When she came down, she had a box in her hand. 'The

father of my child bought me these when I told him I was pregnant,' she said, opening the box. 'They were all he could afford to buy me.' The shoes sat in the palm of her hand. 'The baby never got to wear them.'

Flynn reached for one of them. He took it and examined it, the shoe tiny in his big hands. 'So little,' he said, looking up at her with a smile. 'You gave him up for adoption, why didn't you put them on so he'd have something of yours?'

'Because I wasn't allowed to see him.' She took the shoe back and put both back into the lined box. 'I was fourteen when I had the baby, Flynn.' She shut the box and held it to her chest. 'I'm old enough to be your mother.'

'But you're not!' He ran a hand through his hair. 'Your son is living abroad, I'm here.'

'I know. But his being in Australia has nothing to do with anything.'

'Australia?'

Jodie rubbed her eyes, suddenly so very weary, and it was a few seconds before she noticed Flynn's suddenly arrested expression. It was the first test of their relationship, she wondered if they'd make it. She linked her hands over her still flat belly, glad she hadn't told him. Whether they stayed together or broke up, nothing was going to interfere with their child.

Flynn stood and took a few steps away before turning to look back at her. She'd never seen him look so serious and felt her heart break. 'You're thinking of the reality of that fourteen-year age difference, aren't you? When you're thirty, I'll be forty-four, when–'

He held his hand up, stopping her. 'I can do the maths, Jodie, that isn't what's worrying me.'

But he didn't seem to be able to find the words to explain what was, his face turning ghostly pale in the light that filtered through from outside.

'Sit down, before you fall down, and tell me,' Jodie said. It was better to know, better to feel the pain in one blow.

Flynn sat, and rubbed a hand over his face. 'Do you remember I told you that my parents had a big row, and she told him to take a running jump if he wasn't happy.'

'You said she'd never expected him to take her literally.'

'That's it. That's always the bit of the story people remember.' He shrugged. 'I've told it lots of times, and not once has anyone ever asked me what they fought about. What was so serious that he would pack up and leave.'

Jodie didn't want to ask. She met Flynn's sad, serious brown eyes, and she didn't want to know. The truth was vastly overvalued.

But she couldn't break her gaze and finally, he spoke. 'They had a huge row because Mum changed her mind.' Flynn got to his feet, crossed to the sink, and filled a glass with water. For a second, he simply looked into it, then he lifted it to his mouth and emptied it in two long gulps. He put the glass down and wiped his mouth with the back of his hand.

'I'm adopted, Jodie. The first time... when you said you'd given a baby up for adoption... I tried to tell you but you didn't want to talk about it anymore and cut me off.' He looked back at her then, a wealth of pain in his eyes. 'It's never been an issue for me, so I didn't think any more about it.' He laughed harshly. 'Or I should say, it's never been an issue before.'

He pushed away from the sink and walked to the far end of the room, putting as much distance between them as possible. 'After they adopted me, my parents were supposed to emigrate. The plan was to go to Australia, but Mum decided it would be better to bring me up in the UK. That was what the row was about.'

Jodie stared, her mouth suddenly dry. How many families adopted babies with plans to emigrate immediately following adoption... perhaps a few... how many of those had planned to go to Australia... maybe some. Or none. 'It's just a coincidence,' she said but she saw the truth in his eyes and felt it in her heart. This was why there'd been that instant connection between them. An unconscious recognition between a mother and her son.

'Maybe,' he said.

And Jodie knew from that one word that, regardless, their relationship would never be the same again. 'We can get a DNA test done, it only takes a few days.'

'Okay.' He took a step in her direction, then shook his head and jerked a thumb towards the door. 'I need to get some air.'

He didn't ask if she wanted to come, and he never would again. The crack she'd felt opening under her feet hours before widened, and she felt herself slipping inside. They'd never walk hand in hand to the Italian restaurant again, never stop to kiss, just because. Never lay naked together, hot and sweaty after making love for hours and talk about their future.

Her hands tightened over her belly. What was she to do about her baby? This child of her child.

Struggling in the deep dark pit she found herself in, she had absolutely no idea.

42

Flynn never returned that night. Jodie cried as the happy future she'd planned turned to vapour around her before vanishing like a mist of warm breath on a cold day. The shock of the unbelievable disclosure had numbed her; but the piercing pain of facing the truth would come.

Before she went to bed, she did an internet search and ordered a DNA kit. She had to be sure.

The following day, she worked a twelve-hour shift and returned home a little after 8.15pm, weary in body and mind, tight bands of tension around her head and her chest. She'd sent Flynn a few messages during the day, but she'd heard nothing from him. When she turned the corner into Wilfred Street and saw the house in darkness, her steps slowed almost to a halt. But reality had to be faced. Even with the piercing pain in her chest and in her belly, as if the baby she carried felt the same agony of loss, she had to know.

The pain faded to a deadly heavy ache as Jodie walked from room to room, past tears. Flynn had been in while she was at work. He'd not taken everything... his suits still filled the new wardrobe... but all his other stuff was gone. She filled a glass with water and sat at the table.

It was several minutes before she noticed the note propped against the kettle but she felt no inclination to jump up and grab it. What could it say, after all? There was no way back from this.

Eventually, she stood and picked it up. She unfolded it, smoothing out the creases with one hand while she tried to read the words through tear-filled eyes.

From the first moment I saw you, I felt this amazing connection. I put it down to some romantic notion of love at first sight but I know now it was something more... I think you feel it too. It's best if we don't meet... for a while anyway. Send me whatever I need to do for the DNA test and I'll do it. When we know, for sure, it will be easier.
Flynn

Easier? Jodie barked a harsh laugh and crumpled the page in her hand. Maybe she should have told him about the child she carried... their child. A child with the man she loved, isn't that how she had described it, her pride coming before the almighty tumble into the deep. If DNA proved what her gut told her was true, she was carrying her own grandson.

It was almost funny.

The next few days passed in a blur. She didn't hear from Flynn, had no idea where he was living, her messages to him, read but unanswered.

When the DNA kit came, she sent the enclosed test tube off to his old address and sent him a message to say it was on its way so he could pick it up. It was a simple test, just requiring a sample of his saliva and the enclosed instructions were self-explanatory. She was tempted to write a note to go with it but she didn't. She wouldn't have known where to start and wouldn't have been able to stop writing the stupid things, the *I love you* that still came naturally. Words that were so heart-achingly unnatural faced with what they guessed to be the truth.

A day later, she arrived home to find an envelope with the test tube sitting on her door mat. He had enclosed a note. Three words that made her weep. *I miss you.*

She didn't crumple this one, instead she folded it and put it into the back pocket of her jeans and later that evening, she took it out and read it again. He missed her, she'd missed him for so many years. A bizarre circle that scrambled her brain. She folded the note again carefully, opened the baby-shoe box and tucked it under the tissue paper.

The DNA test went off the next morning. She paid a little more for the express service which guaranteed results within two days. She'd told Flynn it would take a week... it would give her time to adjust before she had to tell him. Either way, she knew she would need it.

She also needed time to decide what to do about the baby. It was early in the pregnancy; if the DNA results confirmed the worst, she had options. Or did she? The thought of getting rid of this child... one conceived in love... was unthinkable. It was her second chance and she wanted it.

Two twelve-hour shifts back-to-back filled her days and made her too weary to think. She was grateful for the temporary escape and arrived home after the second day dreading the four days before she would work again. Exhaustion helped her sleep, but worry woke her early next morning, hours before there was any chance of the post arriving.

She didn't dress, sitting in her robe with mug after mug of coffee waiting for the clunk of the letterbox. Until then, she'd no interest in doing anything else.

It wasn't until ten past eleven that she heard what she'd been waiting for. It took another ten minutes to gather enough courage to get up and take the few steps into the hallway where one single envelope sat on the mat.

She picked it up, brought it into the sitting room and sank onto the sofa, her eyes fixed on the logo on the top right corner – an entwined DNA. It would be a helix of grief if the news was what she expected it to be.

There was only one sheet inside the envelope. The company obviously didn't believe in wasting time: there was no pleasant greeting, no gracious thanks for her custom. Just the results, in stark typescript on the white paper. There was a 99.5% chance that she and Flynn were related.

The page floated to the ground defying the weight of its news. It was ironic: a year ago, had she been told that the handsome, charming Flynn was her son she would have been proud, delighted and relieved. Now she was torn between the feelings for her son and the feelings for a man she'd grown to love, the father of her child.

The house closed in around her, taunting her with glimpses of happy memories, echoes of Flynn's laugh in every corner. When her eyes kept filling, she knew she had to get out. She pulled on suitable clothes, and ten minutes later was heading for Cliffe Fort, head down, hands jammed into her pockets. Unbrushed hair blew in rat's tails around her head, blinding her, strands sticking to her tear-stained face.

Walking brought no relief, the view from the headland across the Thames brought no comfort. She started the long walk home, her feet scraping the path.

The day stretched ahead long and lonely with only grief for company. Ringing Rivka wasn't an option anymore, and the pain of that loss added to all the rest and made her almost choke with heartache.

As she passed a café, the sound of laughter floated out and she stopped and stared through the window. It sounded so like Flynn. She pushed open the door and entered, her eyes scanning, her face falling to see it wasn't him. Of course it wasn't. But it was warm and bustling inside so rather than facing the emptiness of home, she bought a coffee and sat.

43

Victor had continued to follow Jodie despite her threats. It wasn't difficult, he was an expert at fading into the shadows, his features so neutral as to render him almost invisible.

He'd seen Flynn leave a few days before, a strange look on his face. Victor had waited until midnight, the chill numbing his bones, but Flynn had never returned.

Nor did Victor see him the following days. Trouble in paradise again. He wondered if Jodie had shown him the photograph, if Flynn had seen what Jodie refused to acknowledge. Or maybe, they'd simply decided they weren't, after all, right for each other.

Victor had nothing else to do apart from stalking Jodie, but the weather was turning colder, standing for long periods of time becoming increasingly uncomfortable. Her shifts in the new nursing home were erratic so from necessity, he waited on the corner of her road every morning. When she'd not appeared by 7.30am, he knew she wasn't working that day and headed home, returning at ten. If she were meeting her friend in the city, or going shopping, she rarely left before that.

That day, when a little after eleven she left the house in casual clothes, he knew she was heading for a walk. Often, he struggled to keep up with her long, brisk strides but he was in luck and she trudged along, making it easier for him to follow.

Normally, and he'd followed her along this walk a number of times, she'd spend several minutes at Cliffe Fort. He supposed she admired the view from the headland across the Thames and towards the Cliffe marshes or maybe she was struck by the historic importance of the structure itself. Victor thought it was a dump, and the Thames a cesspit.

Unusually, she reached the fort and immediately turned without stopping. Had she been looking up, she'd have stared straight at him, but she kept her eyes down as she faced into the breeze that blew across from the estuary, her hair swirling out behind her.

Victor was cold. He'd not expected her to head out for a walk and he wasn't dressed for the biting chill so it was with a grunt of relief that he saw her stop at a café and go inside.

It was a small café. Unless she kept her head down, she was bound to see him. He hesitated with his fingers grasping the door handle before deciding not only to go in, but to go in and join her.

The café was busy, too noisy for his taste but at least there were tables free. Jodie was ordering at the counter and didn't notice him enter. He stood reading the menu on the whiteboard only a few feet away and watched her. Even from her profile, he could see she looked peaky, her eyes red. She wasn't ageing well, he decided with grim satisfaction. Soon, she'd look as worn and weary as he did.

It seemed to take her an age to order, her head stretched forward across the counter towards the server and he was surprised when she came away holding only a mug. Without looking in his direction, she crossed the café to a table by the window. Victor stood staring until the 'can I help you?' registered and he stepped up to the counter. He ordered a pot of tea and a scone and paid what seemed an exorbitant amount for such simple fare.

It was with a strange sense of inevitability that he picked up his tray and crossed to Jodie's table. She didn't look up so he unloaded his *tray without fuss and took the chair opposite. It was the scrape of the chair legs on the floor as he pulled it closer to the table that caused her to raise her head.*

She didn't appear surprised or angry, as if his arrival were something she'd always predicted would happen. 'You kept following me,' she said, her voice dull.

Victor leaned closer. 'I have to make you understand... to believe.'

Jodie's expression didn't alter. She picked up her drink, sipped it and stared out the window.

Victor sat back with a grunt of annoyance when a young woman appeared with a plate in her hand. 'Here you go,' she said, putting it on the table in front of Jodie. 'I hope toast helps. Morning sickness is the pits.'

Morning sickness? *Victor stared at Jodie, his mouth slightly open, eyes wide. 'You're pregnant?'*

Jodie didn't answer him and turned back to look out the window again.

'This is why Flynn walked out on you.' Victor's lips curled in a sneer. 'I knew he wasn't the man for you. But you don't need to worry, I'll stand by you, the way I would have stood by you with the first baby if I'd been let. We'll simply pick up where we left off.'

Jodie looked at him then. He expected relief, maybe even pleasure, but her face was squeezed into lines of hatred.

'Where we left off? You're a rapist. A monster. I wouldn't let you near my child.' The chair tipped backwards and almost fell as she got to her feet. Without another word she hurried from the café.

Victor watched her go. She'd change her mind. She had to. They were meant to be together. And now they'd have a child to rear.

He'd sat back with his mug before he noticed Jodie's handbag hanging from the back of the chair. With a glance around, he leaned forward, caught it with his long fingers and brought it close. A discreet look inside made him smile. Her house keys.

He knew she'd need him. Here was the proof.

44

Jodie almost ran the two miles to her house and arrived at her front door breathless, sweating, and angry – with herself, with Victor and even with Flynn who was the only truly blameless person, his silly lies not counting.

When she searched her pockets for her keys, she almost screamed in frustration. She'd had a bag, her keys were inside. There was no choice, she had to return to the café. Victor would have seen it, he'd be waiting for her. A smirk on his creepy face.

But when she got to the café both he and her bag were gone.

'I didn't see it,' said the same server who had spilled her secret to the one man in the world she would have kept it from forever.

Victor... he'd taken her bag.

She'd no choice... she never had a choice, too often her life seemed to be taken out of her hands and here she was again, forced to do something she didn't want to do. Victor would be waiting for her in his flat. He would gloat that she needed him and make of it something that it wasn't. He might even think she'd left her bag deliberately. She squeezed her eyes shut, horrified at the thought.

But she was wrong. She walked around to his flat and kept her finger pressed to his bell until it was numb, then stood craning her neck to see if there was any sign of him at the window. She'd been so sure... puzzlement creased her forehead. An even more horrendous thought slammed into her with such force that it rocked her on her feet.

Victor knew where she lived; and he had her keys.

She turned and ran for home, hoping to find him waiting outside, her bag in his hand looking smug and superior. But once again she was wrong and she supposed she should have guessed that the temptation would be too much for him.

Her front door was ajar. She pushed it open slowly and listened. Silence. Two quiet steps and there he was, in the sitting room, on the sofa, the DNA report in his hand, his mouth gaping in disbelief.

He looked up as she stepped through the doorway and shook his head. 'Flynn is your son... our son.'

There was no point in denying it, not with the proof in his hands. She sat opposite and said nothing.

Victor looked at the report again. She saw his lips move as he read the scant details. 'I thought he'd gone to Australia,' he said, looking back to her.

'It appears they changed their mind at the last minute.'

Then Victor asked the question she'd been waiting for. 'And the child you're carrying?'

Jodie didn't answer; she didn't need to. Victor had been following her, he knew there was nobody else.

'Oh, my dear,' he said, 'this is tabloid gold. You're pregnant with the son of your son! I can see the headlines now!' His laugh was loud, raucous, spittle gathering in the corner of his open mouth.

Jodie clamped her mouth shut. *Tabloid gold*? She remembered Victor's seedy bedsit. Money would enable him to rent something far better. How much money would a tabloid pay for the story? The headline would be a tantalising – *Woman expecting child, by the child she bore as a child* or a pseudo-amused *Keeping it in the family*. And her nightmare of a life would be destroyed.

And Flynn? His ego was already fragile; he, too, would be ruined.

And the child she was carrying?

What kind of a future would it have?

Victor stopped laughing and stared across the room. His mouth was suddenly dry and he wiped his lips with the tip of his tongue. 'I'm sorry for laughing. It was a reaction to the shock of the news. And I'm sorry for that crack about tabloid gold. Of course I didn't mean that.' He hesitated, seeing her shuttered face, her narrowed eyes. This was probably all wrong but he needed to say it. 'I've said it before and I'll keep saying it till you believe me. I've never stopped loving you. I'll be here to help you through this.'

There it was; out. He dropped the report on the sofa beside him and waited for her response.

'Fine,' she said. 'But I'd like it if you left now.'

It wasn't exactly the response Victor had wanted, one that would offer him a glimmer of hope, but it wasn't a cry of outraged disbelief either so he took some comfort from that. He stood and went to the front door, Jodie following behind. Outside, he turned to say goodbye to her but she'd already shut the door and he heard the rattle of the chain as it was engaged.

It was a first step, he decided. She needed him now, the rest would come easily.

Jodie's fingers shook as she put the safety chain in place, then she stepped backwards to the kitchen and sank onto a chair.

She didn't believe anything Victor had said: not his profession of love that had been preceded by that lewd licking of his lips, nor his declaration that he hadn't meant what he said about *tabloid gold*. He was a liar, a monster, capable of anything.

Twilight faded to night as she sat and mulled over her dilemma. If she moved, would Victor follow? She could creep away and change her name, but she had a feeling it was a lot harder to do than it looked on TV.

But she had to do something. She had to protect all of them from Victor: herself, the child she carried, the child she'd borne and the man she loved.

It was late before her thoughts focused on that one certainty.

45

Sleep came in short bursts that left Jodie more tired by the morning. She finally went downstairs at seven, made coffee, switched on the TV, and watched an old movie with so little interest that she didn't notice when one finished and the next started.

Now and then, she'd get up for a coffee refill and once, feeling guilty, she made a slice of toast and nibbled on that.

She waited four days before she sent Flynn a text to say the results were positive. There'd been no word from him since he'd left and she had no idea where he was staying. And she still missed him with an ache that was double-edged... one for her son, one for her lover. She switched off her phone after she sent the text, she didn't want the distraction of wondering if he'd reply or not.

Over the four days, the certainty that she needed to do something with Victor to protect all of them had grown. Ideas and plans flitted through her head but most were quickly discounted. Only one promised a final solution but it was radical and she dismissed it, then came back to it... again and again... as being her only choice. She was racked with doubts that she could follow through with such a drastic plan. But it always came down to necessity. Victor had left her no way out. For her second chance to be a success, she had to deal with him.

But to make her plan work, without repercussions, she needed help. It was Friday, the perfect day. She picked up her mobile and pressed a key, hoping that Rivka would answer.

'Jodie, this is a surprise.'

From the tone of Rivka's voice, it wasn't a nice one. 'I'm sorry, I wouldn't have rung but I need your help. Can we meet?'

There was a lengthy silence before Rivka answered. 'You can come around here if you like, Tasha is away at a conference until tomorrow.'

'Perfect. I'll be there in an hour or so.' Jodie hung up before Rivka could change her mind.

~

Less than an hour later Jodie stood outside the apartment block in Bexleyheath. She had spent the journey going over what she wanted to ask her friend. It was risky but she was counting on her. She pressed the doorbell, waiting for the buzzer to release the front door and took the lift to the fifth floor.

'Hi,' Rivka said from the open doorway of her apartment. There was no warmth in her expression, no welcoming smile.

'It's important or I wouldn't have bothered you,' Jodie said and followed Rivka into the apartment. 'You and Tasha doing okay?'

'We're fine.' Rivka waved Jodie to a seat in the open-plan lounge. 'Coffee?'

'No, thanks, I'm good.' Jodie sat, suddenly nervous about what she was going to ask. Was it too much of a risk? 'You said you'd do anything for love. Or more precisely, for the woman you loved. Is that still true?'

Rivka frowned and considered the question as if looking for a catch. 'Yes, it is.'

'I'm pregnant.'

Rivka's eyes shot to Jodie's belly. 'Flynn's, I assume.'

'Yes, of course.' Jodie leaned closer, fixing her eyes on her friend. 'I love him. I'd do anything for him. It's why I can understand you and Tasha. I mightn't like it but I do understand.'

'Good.' Rivka's frown eased a little. 'Is that why you've come, to tell me that.'

'No.' Suddenly anxious, Jodie got to her feet and paced the room. 'I need to tell you a story. You might be a little shocked.' She sat on the sofa, closer to her friend. 'Don't judge me, okay?'

'You're worrying me now,' Rivka said, shuffling away to put some distance between them. 'You better tell me.'

Jodie did, and as she told her tale, she saw her friend's eyes widen, her hand creeping over her open mouth.

'Bloody hell,' Rivka said when Jodie had stopped speaking. 'You can't seriously be thinking of keeping the baby. Have an abortion. You've plenty of time. I'll even go with you.'

'No, I want–'

Rivka stood and spun round to look at her. 'You are crazy. The chances of the child being born with physical disabilities of some sort are huge. I can't remember the statistics... look them up. You can't take that risk. Anyway, bloody hell, your son's child. That's gross.'

'No, it's not!' Jodie rested her hands on her belly and took a deep breath. 'The baby is blameless,' she said in a calmer voice. 'And I'm going to keep it.' She met Rivka's gaze and gave a tentative smile. 'The baby will be fine. That's not the problem. It's the world he's coming into... at the moment, it's not safe.'

Rivka frowned again. 'What are you talking about?'

'Victor. I need to get rid of him. I've come up with a plan but I need your help.'

'Get rid... fuck, do you mean what I think you mean?' Rivka backed away, shaking her head, her hands raised palms outward. 'I don't know who you are anymore. But if you think I'm getting involved in this, you don't know me at all.'

'I know you're a woman who would do anything for the woman she loved, even to the extremes of cutting her best friend out of her life. What I want to do isn't much worse than that.'

Rivka glared at her in obvious disbelief. 'You're not talking about simply cutting Victor out of your life, though, are you?'

'It needs to be more permanent. I have too much to lose; my child, my son.'

'Your lover?'

'Yes, my lover too.'

Rivka sat and rubbed a hand over her face. 'What do you want from me?'

'Victor likes his whisky, I'm planning on giving him some and want something to mix in it. I need to know the best combination of medication to use.'

'I can't believe we're having this conversation! But since we are – digoxin mixed with some morphine suspension would probably be the best bet.' Rivka's frown was back. 'You could have done an internet search to find that out, you didn't need to come here.'

'Yes, I know,' Jodie said. 'But I need someone to get it for me.'

'No way! Seriously, you think I'm going to get involved in this. Get real, Jodie, this is a crazy idea. I'm having nothing to do with it. You must have residents in the home on this stuff... steal it yourself.'

Jodie shook her head. 'They keep a very tight check on medication in Seacrest Manor. They also know about the NMC investigation, I couldn't take the risk.'

'But you expect me to!'

It was time for Jodie to use what she had. 'You'd do anything for Tasha, though, wouldn't you?' She saw realisation dawn on Rivka's face. 'My union rep advised me that I should go to the police with Tasha's confession.'

'She'd be arrested. It would destroy her.'

'It certainly wouldn't be a good career move for a socially mobile solicitor.'

'And you'd do that... to her... to me?'

'What was it you said, Rivka, that you'd do anything for her. Well, I'd do anything for Flynn–' Jodie rubbed a hand over her belly '–and for this baby. Victor is a monster, he'll destroy them.'

'Victor's a monster!' Rivka sneered. 'And your baby – you'll make it into the child of a murderer as well as the grandchild of a rapist. Is that really what you want?'

They stared at one another, knowing that each had crossed a line and there was no turning back.

'Will you get me what I need?'

Rivka looked away. 'You won't need much, only a small amount of digoxin. The morphine isn't necessary, it would make it a more comfortable death, that's all.'

Jodie nodded. 'Can you get me both?'

'It'll take me a few days, I need to be careful.' Rivka got to her feet. 'I'll drop it off at your house on Wednesday.' She crossed the room to the front door and opened it. 'And I won't want to see you again. Ever.'

Jodie stopped beside her and smiled sadly. 'How strange that it should be love that destroyed our friendship. Goodbye, Rivka. You won't see me again.'

46

The following Wednesday, as Rivka had promised, Jodie found a small package on her doormat. There was no note, nothing at all written on either the outside or on the small bottle it contained. Jodie opened the lid and sniffed. It had a slightly medicinal scent but it wasn't overpowering.

She took out the small bottle of whisky she'd bought over the weekend and emptied half down the sink, then carefully, she poured the contents of the smaller bottle into the remainder of the whisky and shook it gently.

Her plan was ready.

The meeting with Rivka hadn't changed her mind, not even the sneering reference to her being as much of a monster as Victor had. It wasn't true – she wasn't a monster, she was a woman protecting her children. *And the man she loved.* The ache hadn't gone away, it hadn't even faded. How could it when the love she felt for the man was so entwined with the love for her child.

And when she faltered, when doubts piled themselves up, one atop the other, it was love that gave her strength.

She dressed carefully. Black jeans, a dark-grey jumper, a

navy raincoat with a hood, and a navy wool scarf. The weather was in her favour; it had been bitterly cold recently and everyone would be wrapped up warmly. The coat pockets were deep. She shoved several paper tissues into one of them and the prepared whisky bottle into the other.

As she walked away from her house she arranged her scarf so that her mouth and nose were covered. Nearer to Victor's bedsit, she pulled the hood of her coat up and tugged it down over her forehead. Between the hood and the scarf, only her eyes were visible.

She pressed Victor's doorbell and waited, keeping her face to the door. It was a long time before she heard movement on the other side but she'd no intention of leaving, the plan was fixed in her mind, she wasn't going to weaken. She couldn't afford to... too much depended on her success.

'Hi,' she said, when the door opened to Victor's pale, furrowed face. She pulled the scarf down. 'Can I come in? We need to talk.' She shuffled from foot to foot. 'It's very cold out here.'

'Yes, of course, come inside.' He stood back to let her pass through but the puzzled expression didn't fade. 'This is a surprise.'

She said nothing, waiting for him to lead her up the stairs. Praying that they'd meet nobody on the way, she followed him, and was relieved when she was safely inside his dingy accommodation.

'Sit down, please,' Victor said, waving to the single chair. 'I'm glad you came. Would you like something to drink? A cup of tea would warm you up.' Victor had obviously decided her visit augured good news, his puzzled expression giving way to one that was smugly satisfied.

'That would be lovely.' Jodie forced a smile. She reached into her pocket for the bottle. 'You mentioned you liked whisky.

Since I don't drink anymore... or very little anyway... I thought I'd bring you this. It's been opened but not much has gone.' She held the bottle forward, keeping her expression carefully neutral.

'You remembered,' he said, taking the bottle. He read the label and smiled. 'It's good whisky too.'

'Maybe I'll have a drop to warm me up. For medicinal purposes. But only if you join me.'

'Medicinal purposes.' He grinned. 'The only reason I drink it too.' He opened a cupboard, took out two small glasses and set them on the table. 'Here you go,' he said, pouring the whisky into each. He handed her a glass and took his own. 'What shall we drink to, my dear?'

Jodie wrapped her fingers around the glass. There was only one thing to drink to at that stage, wasn't there? 'We should drink to love. It's what has brought us to this point after all.'

He hesitated, as if not entirely convinced of her sincerity, his eyes narrowing as she lifted the glass to her lips. 'I suppose it is,' he said, and raised his glass. 'To love.'

'It's quite a smoky whisky,' Jodie said. 'I don't think it will do the baby any harm to have one or two.' She sat on the solitary chair and raised the drink to her lips again.

Victor hovered as if unsure of the next step. Only when Jodie raised her glass once more, did he cross to the bed and sit.

She managed to fill the silence with ramblings about the baby and a few minutes later, lifted her empty glass. 'It's helping to warm me up already.' She poured more into her glass, then got to her feet and walked over to Victor with the bottle extended. His glass, too, was empty. She filled it to the brim. Back in her chair, she lifted her glass again. 'Here's to the future.'

When she put her glass down it was empty. 'That is really good, isn't it?'

Victor drained the second glass.

'Looks like we're going to get merry together,' Jodie said, crossing to fill his glass again.

It took nearly an hour. The whisky was gone. Victor's eyelids were drooping and he'd flopped back on the bed. When he hadn't spoken or moved for several minutes, Jodie got to her feet and edged closer to him.

He was still alive. She could see the barely perceptible rise and fall of his chest. It was going to take longer. The whisky she'd emptied on top of the paper tissues in her raincoat pocket was sending up noxious odours. She pulled them out and flushed them down the toilet in the tiny bathroom. Then she retreated to the chair and maintained her vigil.

Four hours later she stood over his cooling body. She'd given him a painless, comfortable death. It was more than he deserved. But now he was out of her life for good.

There had been no other way.

Love. It was a powerful motive for murder.

47

Three days later, Jodie was lazily stirring a bolognaise sauce when the doorbell rang. She wasn't expecting anyone and looked towards the hallway with a frown. When it rang again, she swore softly, dropped the spoon into the pot and switched off the gas.

From habit, she slipped on the safety chain before opening but when she saw who it was, she closed the door and undid it, the chain catching as she fumbled.

'Flynn,' she breathed, her face lighting with pleasure. If he were equally pleased to see her, there was no sign, his face more serious than she'd ever seen it, dark circles under his eyes, his cheeks gaunt. There was no need to ask why. 'Come in.'

He stepped into the hallway and waited while she shut the door, waiting to be told where to go, a stranger in the house they'd shared for such a short time.

'Let's go into the kitchen,' she said, feeling suddenly awkward. From their first meeting, conversation between them had flowed free and easy. Perhaps there weren't words for their predicament. 'I'll make us a cuppa,' she said putting on the kettle. There was something reassuringly normal about a cup of tea.

Her eyes flicked over him as she took out mugs and a teapot. He looked so woebegone her heart ached. *For her son or her lover.* The thought made her squirm.

'Here,' she said a minute later, putting a mug of milky tea on the table in front of him and sitting with her own.

Flynn sat staring at it.

'I'm sorry,' Jodie said, although she wasn't sure exactly what she was apologising for. So much... too little.

'Yes,' he said and his fingers snaked around the mug. He picked it up and took a mouthful.

'I'm glad you came, I was worried about you.'

He put his mug down with a clunk. 'Why were you worried about me, Mummy?' He immediately held his hands up. 'God, I'm sorry, so sorry. About everything.'

Jodie smiled sadly. 'It's odd, isn't it. We both felt that strange connection from the very beginning, we simply didn't understand what it was.'

'And now we do.' Flynn looked her in the eyes for the first time since arriving. 'Hard to believe, even now when I know the truth.'

'I always imagined you with blond hair and tanned skin running along Bondi beach.' Jodie tightened her hands around her mug.

'Who was my father?'

Jodie knew the question would come. She'd prepared for it, had done some research and found a suitable name. 'His name was Toby Wall. He was a boy in my class. We thought we were in love, you see, but we were kids. His family moved away shortly after and I never heard from him again. I heard later that he'd been killed. One of those freak accidents.' She let that sink in before adding, 'I thought adoption would give you a better life.'

'It wasn't a worse one,' Flynn said, with a shrug. 'I grew up in a one-parent family in the end anyway.'

As would their child. Jodie's face tightened. Flynn didn't know about the baby and she wasn't going to tell him. How could she? He was struggling to cope with her being his mother, how could she add to that by telling him that she was pregnant with his child. He'd probably be horrified. Like Rivka, he might think it gross and insist she have the child aborted.

No, it was better to keep her secret. She expected to hear any day that the NMC case against her had been dismissed. When it was all sorted, she was going to move away. She was thinking of Scotland. It was a long way from anyone she knew. She would leave her old life behind. *Leave Flynn behind. Abandon him again.* 'Where are you staying?' she asked, pushing the heartbreaking thought away.

'A mate's flat. It's not ideal but it'll do for the moment.'

'Why don't you move back in here?' she said, the words coming unexpectedly, surprising herself. She watched as shock, or was it disgust, flit across his face and she hurried to explain. 'It was something we mentioned, remember? If we didn't work out as lovers, we might end up being flatmates.' She smiled at him. 'We never expected it to end quite like this but...'

Flynn frowned. 'Won't it be odd?'

Odd? Living with her ex-lover, her son, the father of her child. 'It won't be for long, I'm thinking of moving to Scotland, but it will give you time to get sorted. Anyway, stay for dinner. I'm making spaghetti bolognaise.'

He didn't reply. Jodie finished her tea in silence and stood to finish preparing dinner. She'd made extra bolognaise for the freezer. It would be enough for the two of them. Ten minutes later, she put a plate in front of him and handed him a fork. 'Enjoy.'

There was nothing said as they ate, the meal so different

from meals they'd shared in the past where each mouthful was interrupted by words.

Flynn finished his, scraping the plate. 'Maybe I could stay for a while.'

'That would be good.' She felt the tension relax a little. It wasn't going to be easy with this man she loved being so near, being so untouchable. It would take time for both to redefine their relationship.

And maybe, she'd reconsider telling him about the baby.

48

As the last refrain of the Dean Martin song faded away, Jodie dragged herself back to the present. If she hadn't stopped for coffee that day, she might never have met Flynn, and she wouldn't have this adorable child to love.

She also wouldn't have been forced into doing something so abhorrent that to this day she trembled when she thought of it. But she'd had no choice: she'd been a mother protecting her children. Victor would never have let them go, would have ruined them, haunted them.

She'd never stopped loving Flynn, she probably never would. But it was getting easier.

'Here you go,' he said, putting a brimming cappuccino on the table in front of her.

He sat and looked towards the door, lifting his hand in a wave. 'Here's Rosie already, I thought she'd be ages yet.'

The dark-haired woman returned the wave, pointed towards the counter and with a small boy's hand still clasped in hers she joined the queue and lifted the boy to see the array of pastries behind the glass.

'Ben wanted a bite of each,' Rosie said with a laugh when she joined them minutes later.

'Just a small bite,' the boy said, as if that was quite reasonable. He scrambled up onto the chair and smiled all around.

The conversation flowed for a while and then, as was often the way, Flynn and Rosie got into a discussion about something domestic. Jodie never minded: she liked Rosie, and if Flynn had to marry someone, she was glad it was her.

Jodie reached across and cut Ben's pastry into smaller pieces. 'There you go, sweetheart.'

'What do you say?' Rosie said to him.

'Thank you, Ganny,' Ben piped up.

Jodie smiled at the child... her darling, beloved child, her second chance.

It hadn't worked out in Gravesend... she and Flynn living together... there were too many memories of happier times. Too many nights when she yearned for him. She knew he saw it... knew, too, that it repelled him. It made her more reluctant to tell him about the baby.

It wasn't until he said he was leaving, only two weeks later, that desperation made her blurt it out. 'I'm pregnant.'

'No!' He'd looked at her appalled, eyes sliding over her in absolute horror. 'You have to get rid of it.'

As if the baby they'd made together was an abomination... a monster. She'd spread her two hands over her belly as if to protect it and glared at him. 'I'm having this baby, Flynn. Our child... my child.'

He'd walked out then and she didn't see him for a few weeks. But he couldn't stay away, not completely, and although he didn't move back in with her, they stayed friends... of a sort... after all, she was carrying his child.

Jodie decided to follow her original plan and make a fresh start. She sold the Gravesend house and rented a smaller one on the outskirts of Glasgow while she looked around for somewhere to buy. Flynn said nothing about her going but he helped her pack and went with her to the train station for her long journey.

'Come visit,' she said to him as he lifted her luggage onto the racks.

He looked at her, tears in his eyes and shook his head. 'I can't.' Then he was gone.

But when she looked out the window, he was there, staring at her. And when the train pulled out, she waved until he was out of sight.

Three weeks later, she was walking towards her Glasgow home and saw him standing on the doorstep, surrounded by several holdalls. And when she saw his handsome face and the confusion in his eyes, she knew suddenly that there was only one thing to do to make everything all right.

The baby was born on time and without fuss. Flynn was with her at the birth, his brown eyes filling with wonder. 'He's perfect,' he said, resting his finger against the child's cheek.

Absolutely perfect. Jodie adored the baby, would have held him all day every day had she had the choice. *Choices.* She'd looked at the beautiful face of her son, then to the handsome face of his father and knew she was right. She had to reset their lives.

So, for the second time in her life, she gave away her child.

A month later, when she bought a house nearer to Edinburgh, she changed her surname by deed poll to Douglas, asked Flynn to move in with her with the baby, and introduced them to her neighbours as her son Flynn, and his son, Ben whose mother had, sadly, passed away. Apart from the occasional comment about Jodie looking so young to be a grandmother, nobody raised an eyebrow.

Not many months later, Flynn said he was moving out and Jodie knew why before he explained. She'd known it would come. Flynn was too handsome and charming to be on his own for long but it didn't stop her heart breaking while she wished him every happiness.

It was Ben who broke into her memories. 'Ganny,' he said, leaning towards Jodie. 'Can I have some of your fluff?'

'Of course you can, my darling.' Jodie pushed her almost empty coffee towards him and put a teaspoon in his hand.

It had been the right decision, Jodie thought, looking around the table. Flynn hadn't been sure at the time but she'd finally convinced him that it made sense. He took their son, their beautiful Ben, and she became what she was always supposed to be. Flynn's mother and Ben's *Ganny*.

Her second chance to make it all right.

Looking around the table, she knew it had worked. Jodie and Flynn had agreed on the need for secrecy to protect their son, and Rosie had never been told the truth. Jodie's name change had been an effective part of the deception – Ben's birth certificate listed Flynn Douglas and Jo Armstrong as the parents.

The need for secrecy… Jodie had never told Flynn the truth about his father. She'd never told him the truth about what she had done. Some secrets needed to be kept.

Jodie looked around at her boys.

She'd killed to protect them.

She wouldn't hesitate to do so again.

THE END

ACKNOWLEDGEMENTS

As ever, a huge thanks to all in Bloodhound Books, especially Betsy Reavley, Fred Freeman, Tara Lyons, Heather Fitt, Morgen Bailey, Ian Skewis and the amazing cover designers.

The writing community is always generous with help and I was fortunate to have had help with some details of the story from the writers Noelle Holten, Anita Waller and Joanna Ward, thank you – any errors are my own!

Support and encouragement as always came from my writing buddies, Jenny O'Brien and Leslie Bratspis to whom I owe thanks and a large glass of wine – some day!

There would be no fun in writing at all, if my books weren't read – so a big thank you to all the readers, bloggers and reviewers who get the word out there.

Facebook is a marvellous way of interacting with a wide audience and I am lucky to be a member of some wonderful groups – particular thanks go to Beverley Ann Hopper of The Book Lovers; Andi Miller of Skye's Mum and Books; Dee Groocock of Books on the Positive Side; and Caroline Maston and Samantha Brownley of UKCBC for continuing support.

And as ever, thanks to the crowd who keep me sane – my wonderful husband, family, and friends.

I love to hear from readers so if you'd like to get in touch, you can find me here:

Facebook: https://www.facebook.com/valeriekeoghnovels

Twitter:
https://twitter.com/ValerieKeogh1

Instagram:
https://www.instagram.com/valeriekeogh2

Made in the USA
Middletown, DE
20 September 2021

48634838R10151